Lock Down Publications and Ca$h Presents

I0666774

SUPER GREMLIN 5
ALMIGHTY DON'T LIKE NOBODY

Written By
KING RIO

Lock Down Publications
P.O. Box 944
Stockbridge, GA 30281
www.lockdownpublications.com

Like our page on Facebook: Lock Down Publications
www.facebook.com/lockdownpublications.ldp

Stay Connected with Us!

Text **LOCKDOWN** to 22828 to stay up-to-date with new releases, sneak peaks, contests and more…

Like our page on Facebook:
Lock Down Publications

Join Lock Down Publications/The New Era Reading Group

Visit our website:
www.lockdownpublications.com

Follow us on Instagram:
Lock Down Publications

Email Us: We want to hear from you!

Prologue

Black Snake Rasp

"S'cuse me, young man. You wouldn't happen to have a line on Millionaire Markio, now would you?"

Jacobi Long, called FBS Longshot by those who knew him from his two drill rap videos that had gone viral early last month, wiped a hand down his face to clear away some of the chlorinated water and swam over to the side of the inground swimming pool, where the raspy-voiced old man stood looking down at him.

The man was so black that you could scribble on his face with a Sharpie and not even see the ink. His calculating gaze and the shape of his head made Jacobi feel like he was staring up at a hundred-year-old man who'd descended from an ancient species of snake. The Stetson hat on his head was the same vermilion red as his silk tie, his spiffy leather dress shoes were dyed a deeper red, and his trousers were black like the blazer he had draped over his left arm. His shirt was pink like the flesh of a salmon, with pearl white buttons and a bronze American flag pinned to the left collar.

"Man," Jacobi said, shaking his wet dreadlocks and blinking, "man, where the fuck you just come from? How yo' old ass got over here that fast? You weren't right here a minute ago."

The old man's laugh was raspy like his voice.

Keck-keck-keck

"You youngstas are all the same. Always so full'a the wrong questions." Wrinkling his unibrow, Jacobi brought his forearms to rest on the ledge and darted his eyes all around the fenced-in yard, searching for his boys.

It was Sunday, the thirteenth of July, 2025. Jacobi's diamond Rolex Sky Dweller wristwatch read the time as being ten minutes past midnight. The fat diamond FBS pendant that hung from one of his four diamond necklaces stood for Fin Ball Shorties. He and three other FBS members – FBS Tay Sicko, FBS Big Keanan, and FBS Baby Lord – had rented the Lincoln Park mansion for the entire weekend. They'd thrown a two-day pool party all day Friday and Saturday in celebration of Tay Sicko's newly released mixtape, *Lord N'em Off 16th,* and the gang had spent thousands of dollars on food, drinks, drugs, and entertainment.

Mostly everyone had left the mansion party at around ten. FBS Tay Sicko and FYB J Mane were performing at The Visionary Lounge, a popular nightclub in the Austin neighborhood on Chicago's west side, and everyone who was hale and healthy had decided to go.

Jacobi's girlfriend, Brazilia, had a bad hangover from too much tequila, so he'd decided to stay at the mansion with her. His best friend, FBS Takeover, and Takeover's younger brother, Jayson, had stayed back with him. So had Brazilia's older sister, Cherish Taylor, and two of the exotic dancers Cherish worked the Prime Shift with at Queen of Diamonds. They were all inside the 18, 000-square-foot mansion, drinking and drugging themselves into a magical daze while blasting *Hollyhood,* the new Mello Buckzz mixtape, at the highest possible volume.

"You can call me Herb," said the jet black old man. "Climb on up outta that water. I just need a few words and I'll be on my way."

Herb took three steps back as Jacobi lifted himself out of the green-marble-lined swimming pool. Herb was bowlegged and stooped a bit but still he had the posture of a soldier.

"You was in the military?" Jacobi asked, rising to his full five feet eight inches and pulling at the drawstrings on his navy blue Amiri swim trunks.

Herb tipped his head in the affirmative. "Did two tours in 'Nam. One of the most distinguished long-distance snipers in American history."

"My pops was in the Air Force."

"Yeah?"

Jacobi nodded and wondered if the old man was wise enough to hear the lie in his words. The warm night air suddenly felt cold on his cork-colored skin. He nibbled at his bottom lip and inhaled haltingly, thinking of the photo the FBI had shared of Herbert T. Harris late last year. That snapshot showed a much younger Herb in a tan military uniform, smiling without showing any teeth, the whites of his eyes like headlights piercing his midnight face. The photo had been shared hundreds of thousands of times across social media, and the Federal Bureau of Investigation was offering ten million dollars to anyone who could help them find and arrest the eightysomething-year-old man who was now standing nose-to-nose with Jacobi Long.

"Your music is shit," Herb said. An abrupt grimace wrinkled his leathery black face. He straightened his spine and then reached back to knuckle a kink out of his ancient backbone. Or at least that's what Jacobi was led to believe. The grimace vanished in the blink of an eye, and Herb's reaching hand, which had gone behind him empty, came back into view with the fingers curled tightly around the butt of a black Beretta pistol. "Where are the Otis Reddings of your generation? The James Browns. That junk you chumps listen to these days is straight up shit. It's no wonder you got shit for brains."

His grating rasp made it sound as if his throat was lined with sand paper that his voice had to slither through before it dropped off his tongue.

"It's a new day, OG." Jacobi started to delve into the many differences between old-school and new-school music, but Herb raised the pistol and aimed the large round hole at the end of its barrel right at his mouth. The threat of death frightened all thoughts of music from his brain. "I, uhhh, I … uhhh… I got his, I got his number saved in my phone. It's right, right over there."

He pointed at one of the chaise lounges that flanked that side of the pool. At the same instant, the music that had been blaring from inside the big white antebellum mansion died, and suddenly the aggressively feminine sound of Mello Buckzz was replaced by the earthly noises of nature.

A thousand crickets creaked and a hundred frogs ribbeted in the vast expanse of healthy green manicured grass that was split right up the middle by the cobblestone walkway which led from the pool to the mansion forty yards away.

In the pool, the water filtration system emitted a low, steady hum. Two inflated flamingos that were floating on the water's rippling blue surface bumped into each other and then spun away from Herb and Jacobi, as if they knew that Jacobi's frail chest would soon be blown right out of his skinny back and couldn't bring themselves to watch it happen.

Herb canted his head toward the cream-colored chaise lounge Jacobi had just pointed at. *Go on*, that gesture said. *I'll be right behind you.*

"Don't shoot me, OG." Jacobi was walking to the lounge chair that had his iPhone and his two rubber-banded stacks of cash resting on his fluffy black-and-gold Louis Vuitton bath towel. "On my dead homies, I ain't on shit. I don't even know you. Whatever you and bro got goin' on, that's between y'all."

"You two share locations?" Herb asked.

"Hell nah. That man got way too much money to be tellin' a street nigga like me where he stay at. Only reason I got his number 'cause my cousin Mya got a baby by him, and we all from the same neighborhood."

"Don't lie to me, boy."

"Ain't nobody lyin'."

"You're FBS. Say so right there on your chain."

"Maaaan, do you know how many niggas claim they FBS now? You think all the Fin Ball Shortiez know Markio personally? That's like sayin' all the Travelers know T-Fly, or all the GDs know Larry Hoover. Markio might've started Fin Ball Shortiez, he might be the founder or whatever, but that nigga ain't in the picture like that. He already made it out the hood. He got shows on MTN, movies and shit. FBS was just his way of reachin' back, but it turned into some'n bigga."

Cautiously, Jacobi picked up his phone. He utilized the facial recognition software to unlock his phone screen. Thumbing his way through the hundreds of names and numbers he'd saved to his list of contacts over the years, he found himself silently praying that one of his boys would pop outside with one of their Micro Draco pistols in hand. Jayson was no shooter, but Montaik Slauson, AKA FBS Takeover, was a real gunslinger. He'd shot more than a dozen rival gang members in the last year alone. A few of them had died.

Jacobi was swiping past the names that started with L when Herb made a sound in his sandpaper throat that might have been a grunt. When he looked back to investigate the grunt he saw that the old man had screwed a sound suppressor into the Beretta. Herb's expression had hardened.

"You must take me for some kinda fool," Herb said. His black leather face spread out in a cold facsimile of a grin. "Yeah, that's what it is. Think I'm some kinda jive-ass sucka."

"A what, nigga? Don't start tweakin', old school. I'm -"

Pyoo.

Herb had lowered the gun so that the fat round hole at the business end of his black cylindrical silencer was trained on Jacobi's hip. The gun recoiled when he squeezed the trigger, and the feel of the bullet smashing through Jacobi's pelvic bone was like being punched in the hip by an impossibly strong boxer.

Jacobi dropped his phone, slapped both of his hands over the hole in his hip, and screamed through clenched teeth as he fell to the ground. The excruciating pain sent forth a salty liquid well of emotion from his tear ducts. He screamed again.

"Think I didn't do my homework? Huh? Huh, Longshot?" Herb sneered. "Markio was here a few hours ago. I saw the video. You put it on your Bookface ... or Facebook. Whatever you call it. Your social media."

"He left, man! He left!" Jacobi cried.

"Where'd he go?"

"Michigan City! It's in Indiana, man. Argh, *shit!* I swear to, I swear to *God*, man! That's all I know!"

Hot red blood gushed out between Jacobi's skeletal brown fingers, coloring the sparkling white diamonds in all seven of his platinum rings. He'd made close to six hundred thousand dollars off the one hundred pounds of exotic bud Millionaire Markio had fronted him, and after paying the $220, 000 he owed, he'd blown over a hundred and forty grand on jewelry and another ninety thousand on a used Lamborghini Gallardo.

Hearing approaching voices, he looked back over his shoulder and saw that Takeover, Jayson, Brazilia, Cherish, and the other two strippers – Gold Body and Sasha the Stallion – were hurrying down the cobblestone walkway with their hands held above their heads. The five men urging them forward had balaclavas covering their faces like SWAT Team policemen and compact assault rifles aimed at the backs of their hostages. The sixth masked person, who was leading the line, was a woman; her lashy feminine eyes and voluptuous hips betrayed her sex. She wore a large black shoulder bag.

"In the water," Herb barked. "All'a ya."

Take and Jayson dropped right into the pool. The girls were slower going. Brazilia hesitated, looking back at her wounded boyfriend until one of the gunmen stepped forward and gave her a violent shove. There was a yelp and a splash. Brazilia surfaced a brief moment later, coughing and sputtering, flailing her golden brown arms. Her big sister pulled her close and they embraced like long-lost siblings.

"Somebody better tell me where I can find Markio," Herb threatened. "Either that or you'll all be goin' to see Little Archie." *Keck-keck-keck-keck-keck.* "I'm sure he'll appreciate the company."

Little Archie was Archibald Wilson, the notably ugly young man whose brains Herb had blown out from a hundred yards away. The shooting had taken place at The House of Lords, Millionaire Markio's sprawling 25,000-square-foot megamansion, which stood at the curved end of a long, cane-shaped driveway just a few blocks north. That murder, committed in the affluent Lincoln Park neighborhood that hadn't seen a homicide in four years, was one of the main reasons why federal authorities were on a manhunt for the elusive Herbert T. Harris.

"Markio's in Indiana," Cherish said. "I don't know where exactly that is, but if you give me some time I can find out the address. I'll get Prinny to tell me where he is. All I know for now is that Alexus flew him to Indiana when you and Whitney Clarrett escaped from those kidnappers in Miami Beach. They thought you'd be out to kill him."

"And oh oh *oh* … How right they were," Herb said, beaming.

He swung his pistol toward the swimming pool and shot Take through the right eyebrow. Blood and brains and a handful of dreads sprayed out from the back of his head, coloring the pool water behind him pink. Gold Body gasped, Sasha and Brazilia screamed, and Jayson's eyes went wide with horror half a second before Herb put a .45-caliber round through his left ear.

Pyoo, rang the silencer; quiet and cute, like a fart from a unicorn.

When Herb turned back around, Jacobi squeezed his eyes shut and waited for death…

Chapter 1

"So what's the word, big cousin? What we on?"

That was Kayshawna Earl, who'd changed her name to Kash when she developed an affinity for the same sex. She was camel-colored and round-faced, wearing a Burberry tee-shirt with matching shorts.

Markio Earl donned a similar outfit, only his high-end designer of choice was Louis Vuitton. The cavernous living room he and his paternal family were gathered in had three gray Italian leather sofas with polished steel frames gilded in real 18-karat gold. The floor was paved in gray marble that had gold veins writhing through it, and the television was a 215-inch widescreen. Oak-framed landscapes that had likely cost the lakefront mansion's billionaire owner millions hung from the dazzling white wall behind the sofa Markio and three of his family members were seated on, and the opposite wall was the glass exterior wall, which overlooked the massive back lawn that led out to the wood-planked pier.

The Dub, Millionaire Markio's 155-foot yacht, stood next to the pier like a miniature *Titanic*, whispering in the gentle waves of Lake Michigan.

"Nothin'," Markio said to Kash as she stood before him with Chief Sosa, his jet black French Bulldog, cradled against her chest. "We ain't on shit. They don't want us at the funeral, we ain't gon' go. Fuck them niggas."

"Don't say that. Mrs. Slauson is just mad that the old man was looking for you when he killed her sons. That's all it is. You know she's a church woman. She feels like every bad thing that happens comes from the devil, and she doesn't want nothin' to do with it."

Markio had no reply to that, so Kash shook her head and walked off to join the younger generation of Earls who were standing in the open doorway of the wide glass door that led out to the shaded rear porch, rocking their bodies to the thrumming bassline of the Nicki Minaj music video that was playing on the huge TV screen.

It had been seven whole days since one of the FBI's most wanted fugitives shot and killed two young men in a swimming pool behind an antebellum mansion in the wealthiest stretch of Chicago's Lincoln Park neighborhood, which had now seen just three homicides over the past decade, all of them perpetrated by Herbert Harris.

Growing up, Markio had always referred to the old man as Uncle Herb. because Herb had been married to Markio's aunt Bone for more than fifty years. Herb had looked just as old when Markio was eight as he did now, thirty years later. He'd always had a military bearing about him – from his finely polished shoes to the razor-sharp creases in his slacks – and he'd never gone anywhere without a big pistol in the glove compartment of his fancy brown El Camino and an even bigger wad of cash in his pocket.

Kash's father, Kevin, and his older brother, Antonio, were seated to the right of Markio. Kevin and Antonio were called Kay and Buck, respectively, and the two of them were busy rolling blunts of exotic weed that Markio would take no part in smoking. He'd quit smoking weed and drinking Lean five months ago, when Uncle Herb escaped from the Mexican drug cartel that had held him captive in Miami Beach, Florida.

One could not afford the luxury of drowsing when there was a government-trained assassin hot on his trail.

Seated to Markio's left was his youngest sister, Shakia. She had the same round face and handsome features, which was why the whole family called her his twin. She wore a form-fitting white Chanel dress that had cost Markio just over seventeen thousand dollars. The .45-caliber Glock pistol she had in her white leather purse was identical to the one Markio had in his waistband. Her thumb and the gold lacquered nail ascending from its cuticle were a rapidly swiping blur on the screen of her iPhone.

"It's on all the news sites," she said. "Here go one from MTN News. 'Funeral services for Montaik and Jayson Slauson, the two young men who were reportedly slain by one of the FBI's most wanted fugitives, will take place today at North Lawndale's 16th Street Baptist Church. The Slauson brothers were partying with a small group of friends inside a Lincoln Park mansion when a team of heavily armed gunmen entered the property through an unlocked door and forced them all outside at gunpoint, where wanted killer Herbert Harris ordered them into a swimming pool and demanded they tell him where he could find Millionaire Markio – New York Times bestselling novelist and critically acclaimed screenwriter of such films as *Red City Blues*, *The Bird Man* and its blockbuster sequel, and *Never Smile Again*. When the group revealed to Harris that they had no knowledge of Markio Earl's whereabouts, the Slauson brothers were savagely executed, their friend Jacobi Long was shot and wounded, and Herbert Harris fled the property with his team of masked gunmen in a black Chevy Econoline that was later found burning on the side of the Dan Ryan Expressway.' Same story on the other sites, for the most part."

Kay scraped a stray grain of weed from the pointed tip of his tongue and said, "I just needed to put out a statement. I don't see why, really – I'm a street nigga, you know; I don't do the politics – but I can understand the need for it from a PR perspective. I ain't posted nothin' on social media since lil bro n'em got smoked last week. She tryna protect my image, but y'all already know what I'm tryna do."

"On gang," Buck said, because the mission they were on went without saying.

Markio was a gangster. No amount of accolades or Oscar nominations would ever change that fact. He was like Curtis "50 Cent" Jackson in that way, creating classic street gems for the small screen and the big screen because he had lived through a lot of those very same scenarios. Only it was different with Millionaire Markio. He was still an active gang member, still a drug-dealer, still a gunslinger. When rival gangs came for him and his Fin Ball Shortiez gang on social media, his idea of trolling them was to send a few carloads of killers to every location his opposition was known to frequent, and a lot of times he'd go himself. The only real difference between the Markio he'd been twenty years ago and the Markio he was today was that he was now a higher-ranking member of the Traveling Vice Lords, and instead of serving twenty-dollar crack rocks to junkies he now had a Mexican drug cartel connect that supplied him with several metric tons of cocaine, heroin, fentanyl, and high-grade Mary Jane every year.

The streets of Chicago were on pins and needles, waiting for a response to FBS Takeover's brutal murder.

Meanwhile, Millionaire Markio and the great majority of his paternal family were gathered here at this incredibly spacious beach house in Michigan City, Indiana, waiting for his sister Mariah and two of her friends to arrive so they all could get the yacht party started. Mariah had planned the outing and all its activities weeks ago, hoping it would get Markio out of the funk he'd been in ever since the May evening when a swarm of FBI and Homeland Security agents raided his Lincoln Park mansion as part of an investigation into the kidnapping of Whitney Clarrett, his ex-girlfriend and the CEO of the Kiss Kosmetics lip gloss empire. Whitney had been missing for two years before Herbert Harris murdered her captors and freed both her and himself from the world-renowned Versace Mansion in

Miami Beach. The famous property was owned by Alexus Costilla, the Texas billionaire whose film and TV companies – the Minority Television Network and MTN Films – had produced all of Markio's movies and TV shows.

Needless to say, that raid had put Millionaire Markio and Alexus Costilla in a precarious situation. The federal government had them under a magnifying glass on a bright and sunny day, simultaneously investigating them and hoping they'd spontaneously combust from the attention.

"Sis just got off the highway," Shakia said, reading a text.

"About time," Markio quipped. "How she gon' be late for an event *she* set up? I tell you about black people."

Shakia laughed. "Get off my sista, maaan," she said. That was her go-to line whenever she heard him say something shady about Mariah. The line worked, because while the three of them shared the same father, Shakia and Mariah also had the same mother. If they were a white family that would have made them Markio's half-sisters, but black families didn't operate that way. In black families, a half-sibling was a whole sibling. Far too many black babies had been torn from the loving arms of their mothers in the early years of American history for modern-day black babies to view each other in a half-light.

"I'll be right back," Markio said, grunting as he rose from the butter-soft sofa. He'd strained a muscle in the back of his left shoulder working out in his home gym a couple of days ago, and the dull ache didn't want to leave. "As a matter of fact, just text me when sis pulls up. I'll be in my room."

Shakia's chin rose and fell, but just barely, the tiniest semblance of a nod. She had already swiped her way to a more engrossing news story: the heartbreaking drowning death of Malcolm-Jamal Warner, the man who'd played Theo on *The Cosby Show*.

Leaving the sunken living room, Markio shot a smiling glance at Chief Sosa, and the dog immediately began wriggling and barking in Kash's arms until she lowered him

16

to the floor. Markio chuckled as the little black dog came running up beside him. They climbed the wide cherrywood staircase together, Markio checking the text messages on his iPhone, Chief Sosa galloping up the steps next to him with his long tongue dangling out of his mouth.

The beach house was an architectural marvel, like something out of a magazine famed for showcasing the homes of the rich and famous. It could have been designed by the same company that arranged the living room. Glass and steel and gray marble and sumptuous leather were all it had to show. There were eleven bedrooms and fifteen bathrooms. Chief Sosa even had his own doggie play room that was filled with tennis balls, toy bones, doggie beds, and other things he could occupy himself with when he wasn't trotting alongside his owner.

Markio had a text message from Tiara "Shmoney Rose" Moore, Chief's previous owner. *How my baby doin???* He'd bought Chief Sosa off her for twenty grand when she quit the reality show she'd starred on and moved into the twenty-million-dollar Los Angeles penthouse she'd won in the divorce from Chris Stewart, star pitcher for the Chicago White Sox.

He good, Markio replied as he and Chief entered his bedroom. He snapped a photo of Chief and sent it to the gorgeous ex-stripper who'd raised him from a pup.

There were two more texts regarding Chief Sosa. One was from Patricia Worthington, the Chicago veterinarian who'd given Chief his annual health exam three days ago, and the other was from Morena Manfield, a registered nurse Markio had met while he and Chief were enjoying a midday stroll along the sandy shore of Washington Park Beach. Worthington's message was that Chief's blood pressure and cholesterol were slightly elevated, but he was in good health. Morena's message was more of a demand:

FaceTime me so I can see that cute little dog you had with you at the beach the other day.

"These bitches love Sosa," Markio said, quoting the drill rapper after whom Chief was named.

His bedroom was larger than most apartments he'd lived in as a child. The walls were the same dazzling white as the walls downstairs, and thick, smog-gray carpeting covered most of the cherrywood floor. The bed was a bountiful California King, draped in rich gray Louis Vuitton linen that the maid, Mrs. Nettles, had fixed in perfection. Four rows of bookshelves lined the wall beneath the 150-inch television. The book collection was eclectic; age-old classics from Aurthor Conan Doyle, Henry Louis Stevenson, and H. G. Wells stood alongside the modern-day works of Stephen King, Sister Souljah, James Patterson, Walter Mosley, and John Grisham. Nine of the novels were written by Millionaire Markio himself.

He sat down on the side of the bed and spent a smiling moment contemplating the FaceTime call to Morena. Chief Sosa went to the cherrywood bedside table, stood up on his hind legs, and pawed at the drawer until Markio slid it open and took out a handful of the bone-shaped snacks his canine's nose had scented. Chief followed that handful of goodies with excited eyes, briefly lowering his front paws to the floor before rising again to rest them on Markio's right knee.

Markio fed him a snack with one hand while with the other he dialed Morena's number. Chief Sosa's healthy teeth were crushing the brown bone to bits when Morena's pretty face appeared on Markio's iPhone screen.

"I hope you don't think I wanted to see you," she said. There was a neon green straw pressed down against the center of her lower lip, which was the same shade of pale pink as the top one. Her skin was so light it was almost white. Her shiny black hair was long, lustrous, and wavy, and she had three nose piercings – one silver hoop in the septum and two smaller silver hoops in the nare of her left nostril. "I'm only interested in Chief Sosa. Where is he?"

Markio switched to the rear camera, showed her that the dog in question was busy devouring what must have been the canine equivalent of a T-bone steak, and then selfishly switched back to the front-facing camera so Morena could look at him while he ogled her sexy features.

"I see you're all over the news this week. *Millionaire Markio.*" She said his name like it was a bad word. Sunlight shone down over the left shoulder of her purple tee-shirt. "How come you didn't tell me you were some famous writer?"

"You never asked." "Yes I did. I definitely did. You told me you were a dog-walker. You didn't tell me you wrote *Red City Blues.*"

"First off," Markio said, "if you walk your dog, you're a dog-walker. Hate to break it to you."

Morena's laugh was almost silent. The sun over her shoulder was momentarily eclipsed by a big-eyed blond who smiled and waved and said, "Hey," before dipping out of view.

"Who the fuck was that?" Markio asked, feigning shock.

Morena's sexy smile broadened. "That's Brittany. Brittany Long. She's a nurse, too. We work together at a GEO Group prison in New Castle, Indiana."

We *did* work together," Brittany corrected from somewhere offscreen. "I'd rather *die* than to go back to that place. My days at New Castle Correctional Facility are *over.*"

"Somone threw shit on her last week," Morena explained. "A cup full of wet, drippy shit. Hit her right in the face."

"Ugh." Markio grimaced.

"Yeah. definitely ugh. She quit after that. She has a cousin here in Michigan City who works as an anesthesiologist at St. Anthony's. Got her a job there. I have an interview at two-thirty to see if I can land their last open nursing position. If so I'll be moving up here with her, because I'm just as sick of that prison as she is."

"Wanna be my nurse?"

Morena rolled her droopy brown eyes and looked away from the camera. Her focus went to something in front of her. Whatever it was was low to the ground. Maybe a child, or a dog. There was a minor case of acne going on behind her neatly layered makeup, but Markio thought her face was just as sexy as the rest of her. She had a petite frame that was anchored by a big round butt. When he first laid eyes on her she was rising out of the lake in a plain white bathing suit, water dripping from her limbs as she trudged forward onto the sandy shore. Her beautiful light brown eyes had immediately locked on to Chief Sosa, who'd been barking at the receding water and then running away when it came washing back toward him.

"Awww, such a cutie," she'd said, and her fawning intonation got Chief to staring at her. When she started toward her beach chair, Chief fell in step behind her, no doubt hoping his cuteness would be rewarded with something tasty from her bag.

Markio had ogled her jiggly ass as she walked to her chair, and somewhere along the way he'd fallen in lust.

Maybe it was even love.

"I'm serious," he said, feeding Chief another bone. "My shoulder all fucked up. Few weeks ago me and my son was both sick, and he ain't even three yet. I need a full-time nurse." *Preferably with an ass that jiggles like yours*, he thought but didn't say.

Morena lifted her gaze from whatever she'd been staring at and eyed him dubiously. Her straw moved to the corner of her mouth and pressed down there, giving her pink lips a virgule slant. Markio had time to wonder if her eyes were always that droopy or if she was just high on something. Then she said, "Don't play with me … sir. I have financial responsibilities. School loans, child care, rent, groceries, credit card bills. And so on and so on. I'm making fifty-five grand plus benefits every year at the prison, and if I land this hospital position my pay will go up to *sixty*-five thousand."

Her voice was tight, which wasn't all that surprising. President Trump's senseless tariffs had raised prices on everything from food and liquor to car parts and household cleaning products, and single mothers like Morena Manfield were feeling the bite. Markio had no intention of letting her get away from him. The ostensible reason for this choice was easy to understand: in the middle of an unprecedented crisis, with a highly skilled military sniper hot on his trail and the federal government investigating him for allegedly masterminding his ex-girlfriends' kidnapping, he needed all the help he could get. The true reason, barely submerged, was that he felt alone. He'd been single since January, when he and Kamari White – the dark-hued, thickly-built fashion model Rihanna had recently selected to rip the runway in Fenty X Savage lingerie at this year's Paris fashion week – had called it quits after two months of dating. He'd had a dozen or more flings in the five months since Alexus Costilla put him up at this grand beach house, but nothing serious. He was a year and a half away from forty. He was ready for serious.

"I wouldn't dare play like that." He cleared his throat. "Not about no business. You come work for me, take care of me and my son and my people, and I'll pay you eighty thousand, plus benefits."

"I'ma need that in writing, Mr. Dogwalker."

"Deal. Where you at? I'll come and get you right now. We're about to have this yacht party, and I can't even swim. Might need you to resuscitate me."

Again she silently laughed. It was a beautiful thing to observe. Her eyes were so light brown that they were almost clear, and they became less droopy as the mirth kicked in like a rush of adrenaline, widening as if he'd said something shocking.

"You're funny," she said.

"I just talk shit and swallow spit." Markio chuckled. "I'm from Chicago. That's all we do."

"Yeah. That, and shoot people."

Markio wrinkled his brow and was considering a defensive response when the bright-skinned beauty spoke again.

"We're in line at the Dairy Queen on Michigan Boulevard. Know where that's at?"

Markio smiled. "I'm on my way," he said, and ended the video call.

Chapter 2

"So tell me," William Titus said, twisting the cap off a cold, dripping bottle of Bud Light, "how can the old man afford all this? I mean, I did two tours in Afghanistan, and I know every military pay grade there is. There's no way he was able to save up enough dough to pay us all a hundred grand up front and still take care of all our expenses." He shook his balding head. "No way."

"It's Harmonique Evans," said Kolita Pierre. "She was engaged to Baby Stone, Herb's nephew, when he was gunned down outside of her designer clothing boutique. Our narcotics division and the DEA were building a case against Baby Stone right before he was killed. One of the Black P. Stones from out near Hyde Park got busted trying to deal twenty-one kilos of coke to an undercover, and he'd agreed to wire up on his connect, which of course was Baby Stone. It's estimated that he'd stashed away over ten million dollars in cash before he was killed. The investigation died when he died, and Harmonique disappeared with the money. She's been using it to get back at Markio ever since."

It had been more than a decade since Kalita and her family left Port-au-Prince for the broken promise of America. Even so, her Haitian accent remained prominent, sprinkled over her every word like black pepper on white grits. Her skin was dark and her face was round like a pie. Her naturally thick hair was oiled and braided into a wandering maze of cornrows, the diamond studs in her earlobes weighed four carats each, and she'd painted her lips

23

red like her toenails and fingernails. She wore a yellow crop top with "Don't talk to me, I'm on vacation" emblazoned across the chest in shimmery silver sequins. Her white denim shorts were stringy at the hem and barely acquainted with the lower swells of her meaty derriere. She was a nose hair under five and a half feet tall, and she had the kind of body that made Black women on social media famous: nice tits, a small waistline, and a very big butt.

Kolita sat in the armchair by the front window, with her bare brown feet resting on a soft leather settee in front of her. It was the condo Herb had rented for them, a nice fourth-floor unit at Michigan City's Marriott Hotel with plush slate-colored carpeting and fresh off-white walls. The view was of the four-lane road that led into the city from the highway: a gas station at the catercorner, an IHOP and a sleazy white-and-turquoise motel at the other.

Bill shook his head and swigged his bear. He wore thin-framed eyeglasses and had a receding hairline. He was tall, built like an athlete, and his left arm, from shoulder to wrist, was a sleeve of tattoos. He wasn't smiling now, but usually he was. Smiling and laughing. Bill Titus was the coolest white man Kolita had ever met during her three-year career as an officer with the Chicago Police Department.

"I can't believe we're actually working for this guy," he said. His eyes were on the widescreen television – the two of them were binge-watching *Chicago PD* – but his mind was clearly elsewhere. The annoying fly that had been evading them for the past four days buzzed past his face. He ignored it. "Herbert Harris blew up a fucking Bentley Batur, a two-million-dollar car, right in the middle of Streeterville. For Christ's sake, Oprah used to stay right up the *street* from there!"

"A million dollars each when this is all said and done," Kolita said, picking a blue speck of lint from her white denim shorts. "That's the only thing that truly matters. Whenever we decide to retire, we'll be set. Our families will be well taken care of."

"Yeah, but what if Harris is arrested before he can give us the money? What if he implicates us to get himself housed in a lower-level facility? Have you thought of that?"

"I have. He won't do any of that. Herbert Harris is a soldier. If you stay on his side, he'll never turn his back on you. He wants Markio dead because Markio put a million dollars on his nephew's head, and that bounty got his nephew killed. All we have to do is locate Markio and pass the location on to Harris. Then we'll be millionaires and Harris will probably relocate to Cuba, or Canada, or Mexico. Shit, I wouldn't care *where* he went. Bottom line is, we'll be back in Chicago with a million dollars each. That's good enough for me."

Bill heaved a sigh and drank from his beer. His reluctance was understandable. He and Kolita Pierre were ordinarily good cops. They were members of the Community Safety Team, or CST, which was a group of CPD officers that patrolled different areas of Chicago on an as needed basis. Daily, their supervisors assigned them to whichever areas of the city that required additional police presence at that particular time. Mostly they were assigned to crime-ridden districts where retaliatory gang violence was expected, usually after some big-time gang leader or rap star was slain by his "opps," but every once in a while they were called in to assist in a drug raid. They'd seen thousands of dollars in drug money piled inside shoe boxes and backpacks and lying out on coffee tables, and not once had they stolen a single dollar.

But this was different.

This was *millions* of dollars.

One million dollars for each of the six SCT members who'd volunteered to help the octogenarian war veteran track down and kill Markio Earl.

There was also the added bonus of all the cash and jewelry Kolita had taken from the men and women they'd held at gunpoint at the Lincoln Park mansion last Sunday. The cash alone had amounted to a little over one hundred and eighteen thousand dollars. Split six ways that was almost twenty grand a piece. Best of all, the guys had foolishly allowed her to keep all the jewelry. She'd relieved Cherish Taylor - one of her favorite reality TV stars - of not just the extra large Gucci shoulder bag she'd dropped the stolen merchandise into but also a diamond Chanel wristwatch, a diamond Cuban-link necklace, and three diamond Tiffany bracelets, all of which she wore now (minus the *CHERISH* name pendant, which she'd thrown out the window of their rental car en route to Michigan City).

"I don't know," Bill said, after a time.

"I *do* know," Kolita replied, somewhat snappishly. "And do you know why? Wanna know why I think this is the greatest move we'll ever make? It's because the Trump administration just had their ICE agents arrest my law-abiding father and deported him back to Haiti, where the president was assassinated and the street gangs have taken over. It's because your wife is pregnant with twins, and if you think your pockets are strained now with four kids and a wife to feed, wait until you slide two more chairs up to that dinner table. A million dollars will not only take care of those babies, but it'll also get you that brand-new Ram truck you've been drooling over. A million dollars will get my father a really good immigration lawyer, and I'll be able to move my family out of Haiti, get them situated in a nice neighborhood somewhere in Jamaica. That is my dream. If you want out, go – go go go – but don't you dare try and stop me."

Kolita had more to say, a lot more, but she didn't want to come off sounding like the poor woman from the *Set It Off* movie - *I need this money, Frankie!* - so she went quiet and just stared at Bill Titus. For a while he stared back, his eyes hard orbs behind the lenses of his eyeglasses. His cargo shorts were tan-colored, and he'd torn the short sleeves off his tight brown tee-shirt, which had DON'T TREAD ON ME, some sort of threatening military slogan, imprinted on the chest in bold black lettering.

The spell of silence was broken by the bothersome fly.

It flitted past Kolita's face and bumped her bottom lip before soaring high and disappearing from view.

She jumped up from the armchair and ran in place, spitting and playing her lips like a violin. Bill started laughing.

"It ain't funny!"

"Uh, yes, it is. It's very fuckin' funny."

Kolita didn't want to laugh with him, but she did. That goddamn fly was so good at attacking and then vanishing that they had to laugh. Her eyes rolled left and right, scanning the air around her head. She wouldn't find the bug; of this she was certain. She imagined the pesky, shit-eating insect resting under one of the sofas, rubbing its ugly little stick arms together in triumph.

Scooping up her red suede Madewell purse and slipping into her yellow-and-white leather sandals, Kolita said, "I'll just wait on my date outside, because right now I'm tempted to open fire on that fly, and I'd hate to have to pay for the damages."

Kolita's date was Juan Ashland, a man who was called Juan-G or Loochie by the locals. She'd met him last night at Stevie Lou's, a local nightclub. He'd noticed her sitting alone at the bar and swaggered over to introduce himself. Juan was tall, slim, and handsome, just her type, but most importantly he'd mentioned that he and Millionaire Markio were friends. "Millionaire Markio?" Loochie had smiled at a realm of memories Kolita wished she could see. "That's my *bro*. Shit, we used to damn near live together. That was m nigga when he was Hundredaire Markio."

Kolita was remembering Loochie's suave, golden laugh, and reaching for the door handle, when Bill said, "I'll be down at that Anytime Fitness. Couple of girls I met in there who claim to know our target. See what I can get out of them."

"Text me," Kolita said, and she was out the door.

Chapter 3

Only the hood lid of Millionaire Markio's Rolls-Royce Phantom was black. Everything else was white. The exterior paint, the interior leather, the rims. White, white, white. Which went perfectly with the All-White theme of the yacht party.

Markio sat in back while Shakia drove. He sipped at his chilled bottle of Fiji water and kept his eyes on the foremost windows, as the rear ones had hand-sewn white leather curtains that he kept closed to keep the outsiders from seeing in. his familial security, Kay and Buck, tailed him in his more outdated 2018 Phantom. Even the hood on that one was white.

The two Rolls-Royce created a spectacle as they sailed down Michigan Boulevard. Wide-eyed motorists moved forward in their seats to look. Stunned pedestrians stopped to gawk and point their smartphone cameras. One young Black woman in a dirty gray minivan full of screaming children made an illegal U-turn and weaved around a white Prius to get next to the two white Phantoms.

"This thirsty ho goin' kill somebody," Shakia commented.

"I still can't believe that old-ass nigga killed Jayson and Take," Markio said, but his twin didn't hear him. Young Thug's "Money On Money" was playing from the Phantom's high-tech sound system, and Shakia, a music junkie, had turned it up loud.

She lowered the volume two or three octaves and said, "Huh? Twin, you say some'n?" She eyed him in the rearview mirror.

Markio shook his head in a gesture that wasn't really a lie. He'd been thinking out loud, and now a part of him was grateful that Shakia hadn't heard him. He wanted to keep his father's side of the family as far away from Herbert T. Harris - that prehistoric Devil who'd infiltrated Markio's mother's side of the family through marriage – as he could possibly keep them. No one was safe with old Uncle Herb prowling the Midwest streets. Absolutely no one.

He regretted ever going to FBS Tay Sicko's mixtape release party in the first place. Had he not gone there himself, the Slauson brothers would still be alive, not being lowered into the earth while their closest relatives watched through teary eyes. FBS Longshot would probably be standing in a recording booth, creating his own mixtape to go along with the two hot videos he'd dropped in early June, but instead he was convalescing in a hospital bed at Northwestern Memorial, with screws and metal plates holding his hip together and an intravenous drip of morphine numbing the pain. Word on the street was that Sasha the Stallion, a cast member on the hit reality TV series *The Real Baddies of Chicago*, was so traumatized that she'd gone and checked herself into a mental health facility.

Markio kept reminding himself that he'd *had* to be there. Not just for Tay Sicko, but for FBS as a whole. Every member of the Fin Ball Shortiez played a role in Markio's multi-million-dollar drug empire. He gave out diamond Cuban-link chains and frosty FBS pendants to those who killed for him, an incentive program that had turned a few dozen hungry young Black men into cold-blooded murderers. He rewarded the loyal men and women who helped him get rid of his drug shipments with nice cars and lump sums of cash. He'd even made thespians out of some of his more inspired FBS members, giving them small but notable roles in his films and TV dramas. He offered paid studio sessions to those who wanted to pursue music careers, he paid college tuitions for those who possessed more scholarly aspirations, and he'd also paid for two weddings, three honeymoons, seven funerals, and too many court fees, attorney fees, and commissary fees to accurately remember. He supported Fin Ball Shortiez because Fin Ball Shortiez supported him.

And yet he still regretted going to that party.

He picked up his iPhone and scanned through a few news sites. There was nothing new on Herbert Harris. The old fuck had shown his face just long enough to ask a few questions, kill a few young men, and vanish. Just like he'd done in the Vietnam war more than half a century ago.

After checking the news Markio went to his text messages. He always had new text messages. There was one from his mother saying good morning but really meaning she was bored and needed an ear to gossip into; one from Nikkia Staples, the ex-girlfriend of his who was also his lawyer, saying that CNN was offering him a prime time interview with Anderson Cooper to hear his side of the story regarding the Slauson brothers' murders and the investigation into Whtiney Clarrett's kidnapping; his cousin Jarvon, AKA Slime, had texted saying the private jet he'd chartered from Baton Rouge to Chicago's O'Hare International Airport had landed, and that he was on his way to Michigan City.

Markio texted his mom back first, a simple *Good morning* reply, even though it was now half past noon. His reply to Nikkia was stern: *That's a hard no.* He didn't believe in making public statements against his enemies, no matter how old they were. Those opinions were kept between him and the upper-echelon Fin Ball Shortiez, who would then, adhering to the Vice Land gang's strict chain of command, pass that information down to lower-ranking members who would sand out teams of shooters to resolve the issue.

He was replying to Slime when another text message came in. This one was from Loochie, an old associate of his from Gary, Indiana. Every once in a while he'd have someone deliver fifty or sixty pounds of exotic bud to Loochie, and Loochie never had any trouble getting it all sold and paying what he owed.

The text message read, *Bro where you at? Got this thick lil Haitian bitch say she wanna meet you.*

Markio knitted his brow. The last Haitian he remembered dealing with was Voltaire Muck, a leader of the notorious Zoe Pound gang. Voltaire and a crew of his South Florida dreadheads had robbed one of Markio's stash houses for a few million dollars' worth of product, and Markio, with the assistance of Slime, had gunned Voltaire down in the Southgate Apartments housing complex, right here in Michigan City, Indiana.

He was contemplating a dismissive reply when Shakia shut off the music and said, "That's Dairy Queen right there. Which one of these bitches we comin' to pick up? It better be that thick-ass yellowbone in them low-rise jeans, 'cause she bad as fuck."

It was definitely the thick-ass yellowbone in the low-rise jeans.

There were maybe fifteen people in the parking lot that flanked the single story redbrick building. Roughly half of them were walking towards the long, serpentine line of waiting customers on the sidewalk in front of the building, while the other half walked towards or lingered around their vehicles, licking sweet cream from spoons and cones to combat the sweltering summer sun.

Morena was standing behind a silver-colored Kia Telluride, her and her big-eyed blonde coworker. Those big blue eyes got even bigger as she and Morena watched the two big Rolls-Royces come cruising into the parking lot. Morena stopped licking the cold white bliss from the top of her cone and smiled. Her eyelids widened a bit, and for a very short moment there was no droop.

"That's her sexy ass," Markio said. Joyful air swelled his lungs. "Pull in right next to that Kia truck. Let me pop my shit."

He had forgotten all about the text from Loochie.

Chapter 4

Morena was still smiling when Markio pushed open his rear passenger side door and climbed out into the suffocating July heat. Her nearly translucent brown eyes had gone droopy again, but her smile spanned half the width of her gorgeous face.

"I think that's so dope," said the blonde. "The way the rear doors on a Rolls-Royce open backwards. How much did you pay for that car? Or did you lease it?"

"I don't lease cars, lil mama. I paid half a ticket for this, plus another one-fifty to bulletproof it. Same with the other one."

He saw from the corner of his eye that the slender young white woman was wearing tight little black shorts and a small white tee with an image of a black Santa Claus on the front, but he couldn't make out any details, because his focus was on Morena.

"Not bad for a dog walker." She blinked and smiled and licked her ice cream. "I might need to switch professions."

"I do a'ight."

"Did you really write *The Bird Man*?"

"The books or the movies?"

Morena folded her arms across the chest of her Baltimore Ravens tee, which was purple like the ankle socks sticking up out of her white-and-purple Nike Air Force 1's. "Both," she said.

"I wrote all seven of the books. As far as the movies go, I did a rewrite of the first screenplay, so I'm listed as the co-writer on that one. But I wrote the second movie myself. *Red City Blues*, too. That was all me."

She stared into his eyes and he stared at her lips. They were the pale pink hue of thinly sliced salmon fresh out of the sea. Markio wondered if her clitoris and labia held the same color. He licked his own lips at the thought and flicked a glance at his wristwatch - a custom diamond Patek Philippe that had cost him $300, 000.

"It's one o'clock," he said, feeling a few beads of salty perspiration seep out of his forehead. "Yacht party about to start. We gotta slide."

Brittany the Blonde gasped. *Yacht* party?" Markio looked at her and saw that the black Santa on her shirt was actually Gucci Mane in a festive red Santa hat. *East Atlanta Santa*, read the caption beneath his grinning image. "Did he just say a *yacht* party? Well, bend me over and fuck me with af fucking chainsaw! Amanda picks the perfect time to ask me to go and pick up her snotty-nosed little, little *carpet* crawlers from daycare. Shit on my mother's grave."

Markio chuckled so long it could have been ruled a laugh, and Morena actually did laugh. Letting out a mirthful shout beforehand and holding her cone out sideways in front of her to keep the melting cream from dripping down over her fingers.

Morena went around to the passenger side of the Telluride and was coming back around with a big blue tote bag hanging from her shoulder when the homely young woman in the dirt-laden gay minivan full of kids whipped up behind the Kia and threw open her door.

Kay and Buck popped out of the second Phantom, both clutching high-caliber Draco pistols, but there was no need for alarm. The woman tussled with her seat belt and then stumbled out from behind the wheel with a paperback novel in one hand and a black gel ink pen cinched between the first two fingers of her other hand.

35

Her dark brown eyes were warm and friendly. They were the eyes you'd see in the eye sockets of a veteran yoga instructor; how she maintained such a placid disposition with all the chaos taking place in the rear seats of her vehicle was beyond a man's comprehension. Her tee shirt hadn't been white in a long time. She wore gray sweatpants with beige piping down the sides of AKOO embroidered across one thigh, and they were even more stained than the tee. Yet and still, Markio got the feeling she was a really good mother. Her kids looked clean and healthy, and her smile was much too warm and genuine to be hiding any ice behind it.

"Markio," she said. "Millionaire Markio. Oh my God. You don't know how hard I been lookin' for you. Black Reggie told me you had moved back here from Chicago months ago, but ain't nobody seen you. I was workin' at the bakery until a few weeks ago, and I had all the girls hooked on your book. Especially this series." She held up the book in her hand. It was *Snow Dance 2: Cartels and Customs*, the second novel in an urban fiction trilogy he'd released a few months back. "You mind signing it for me? My name's Twanika, by the way. Twanika Marsh. You can just put Nika."

He held the book against the back of the Telluride and wrote a nice note thanking both Twanika and the women at the bakery. He had just finished scribbling his signature and was handing the book back to its owner when Brittany climbed into the SUV and drove off. Then he and Morena were in the backseat of his Phantom, riding back to the lakefront mansion on Beachwalk Lane.

"Brittany's hilarious," Morena said.

"Too funny," Markio concurred.

"She says crazy shit like that all the time. Sometimes I stay away from her just to keep my stomach from hurting. You can't help but to laugh." Those beautiful light-brown eyes darted to Shakia. "Hey, up there. I'm Morena."

"Shakia," Said Shakia. "You a badass bitch. I see why you got my twin all googly-eyes. You a whole jackpot."

Morena giggled. "Thank you," she said, studying the Phantom's rich leather interior. "Oh my God, this is so nice. I've never been inside an actual Rolls-Royce. I didn't know they were so ... roomy. Roomy. Yeah. A lot of space."

"This the extended wheelbase edition," Markio informed her.his phone buzzed in his pocket. He took it out without looking at it. "It's more spacious than the regular one."

Morena nodded her understanding. With the sun out of her face, Markio could see that the whites of her eyes were a roadmap of squiggly red veins. She smelled like good perfume and vanilla ice cream, the latter of which she was still licking from inside her cone. Two thin gold necklaces clung to her gracefully lean neck. It was clear that she was not wearing a bra; her breasts, full and firm, had nipples that pointed upward like thorns on the stem of a rose. A trickle of cream tried to escape the corner of her mouth, but her tongue swung out and snatched it up.

"Why is that old man after you?" Morena asked the question while investigating the DQ napkin she had wrapped around the lower half of her wafer cone.

"He thinks I paid somebody to get his nephew killed." That was about as close to the truth as Markio was willing to get.

"Did you?"

"Hell nah. Baby Stone was like my cousin. Herb been married to my auntie since before I was born, so that made his family a part of my mama's family. I mean, Baby Stone did owe me a couple dollars before he got smoked, but it wasn't nothin' to spill blood over."

That was an outright lie. Baby Stone had actually owed Markio more than eight *million* dollars, a debt he'd refused to pay, and so Markio had put a million dollars on his head. Slime had collected the bounty.

SUPER GREMLIN 5 | KING RIO

Morena was silent for a moment. After two more buzzes from his iPhone, Markio took advantage of the lapse in conversation to check his notifications.

Mariah and her two friends had arrived at 2212 Beachwalk Lane, and she was irritated that Markio and Shakia weren't there.

Slime's text said he should be pulling up to the beach house in no less than twenty-minutes.

Loochie's message was just a series of question marks.

"I am so not dressed for a yacht party," Morena said, after a long contemplative moment. "What kinda yacht is it, anyway? Is it yours? Does it have a name?"

He nodded and wet his lips. "Yeah, it's mine. It's a hundred and fifty-five foot boat. Got a heated Jacuzzi, a lounge that kinda looks like a small nightclub, four Jet Skis, a swimming pool. Twelve bedrooms - they call them cabins - plus room for the crew. I named it *The Dub*, after a hood in this city I used to kick it in when I wasn't in Chicago. It's on the west side, right after you cross the train tracks behind the Lighthouse mall." his voice went low on that last word, and his eyes went wide. Had that moment taken place in an animated film, a lightbulb would have flashed on above his head.

He turned to Shakia. "Sis, turn left up here. We gon' take Eighth Street all the way down to The Lighthouse Mall. They got a Gucci outlet store. We need to get Morena a swimsuit."

Morena smiled and bit a chunk out of her ice cream cone.

Markio picked up his smartphone. To Mariah he texted, *Chill out, lil lady. One quick stop and we'll be there.* To Slime he texted, *I'm on my way to the Lighthouse Mall. Just meet me there.* He copied, pasted, and sent the latter message to Loochie. Then, on an altruistic whim, he messaged his guy Black Reggie: *Bro, you know Nika? Twanika Marsh? I need you to take her $25, 000. And that ain't no typo, I do mean twenty-five thousand dollars.*

"Oh my God, you are so kind," said Morena. She'd been putting her peripheral vision to use, watching his phone from the corner of the nearly squinted eye.

"She needs it." Markio pocketed his iPhone, unpocketed his wave brush, and began brushing the neat rows of waves on his scalp. "Black women like her, they need all the help they can get."

Morena's wide smile shone on him like the beaming sun in the clear blue sky above. She took another nibble from the rim of her cone and shook her head, and Markio thought his day was going pretty good.

Had he known what was to come, he'd have had Shakia turn back and drive to the beach house, and he'd have ordered the crew on his yacht to get him and his family as far away from Michigan City as possible.

Money can do a lot of things for a rich man - most things, you might argue - but unfortunately, it can't predict the future.

Chapter 5

In Chicago, standing at the massive floor-to-ceiling window in the capacious living room of her forty-eighth floor Streeterville condominium, Whitney Clarrett squinted against the blinding easterly sunshine, her obnoxiously long faux eyelashes fluttering as she did it. Before her lay an awe-inspiring view of Lake Michigan. She wore a curve-hugging, ankle-length blue dress over blue mesh pumps. She was a hundred and sixty-three pounds; forty-two pounds heavier than she'd been when Herbert Harris shot down their captors and freed them both from Miami Beach's historic Versace Mansion, but still thirteen pounds lighter than she'd been before she was kidnapped from the parking lot of a west side Chicago strip club.

She had been brutally raped by two of Markio's goons (sure, she had thoroughly enjoyed being nearly split in two by the first rapist's horse-sized dick, but a rape was a rape). The second man that raped her had afterwards tortured her by shoving a curling iron up her pussy and plugging it into the wall socket.

Then a team of heavily armed men in camo gear had stormed into the basement she was being held in, screaming that they were with the Chicago Police Department, and for one hopeful moment Whitney thought she was saved. She had fainted from the intense pain in her womb, but she had a certain amount of relief in her features whether mental lights went out. She was confident that she would soon find herself lying safe in a hospital bed with clean white linen and a fluffy white pillow behind her head. The rich, nostalgia-inducing aroma of cleaning chemicals and the underlying stench of dying humans would be in the air. A detective in a white shirt and light gray slacks would be standing there next to her bed with his sleeves rolled up and his pocket-size notepad in hand, asking her what she remembered about her kidnappers.

But no, that hadn't been the case at all.

That hopeful dream became a deepening nightmare.

When she regained consciousness some time later – Hours? Days? Weeks? She had no way of knowing – she was drugged up and in a fugue state, not even aware of her own identity and wanting nothing more than to flee from the big empty room she was in. But there was no escaping Hell. Her right leg was shackled to an unyielding corkscrew in the floor next to her cat. A steady rotation of masked Latinos and a few Latinas with big pistols on their hips sat in one corner and watched her day and night. She was given three bottled waters every morning, but there was never any consistency when it came to meals. Sometimes she was fed twice in a day, sometimes she was only fed once, and some days she wasn't fed at all. The pail she was given to piss and shit in wasn't unlike the plastic buckets her children had used as molds to build sand castles at the beach when they were little. When her captors grew tired of dumping that bucket and bringing it back, they started shackling her ankles together and walking her to a bathroom across the hall, with a black bag over head so she couldn't see left or right in the hallway. She'd screamed for help during five or six of those short walks. Each time she was tased into submission.

Whitney closed her lashy eyelids and shook away those dark and troubling memories, letting hte hot sun warm her face. The human mind and body are incredibly resilient. Over the past five months, with the aid of medical-grade marijuana all throughout the day and a few glasses of red wine every evening, she had cleared to keep those traumatic memories in the distant recesses of her brain. Her gynecologist, Dr. Melissa Cambridge, had helped her regain sensation in some of the vaginal areas that red-hot curling iron had burned away. She saw a severe trauma specialist once a week, and her doctor had prescribed her to thirty-milligram Percocet tablets, to be taken twice a day. Her three daughters had moved in with her, and for a few months they'd stuck around to shower her with their love and laughter, but now only Joselyn, her youngest, was left.

There was also the money.

Whitney Clarrett was now rich beyond her wildest dreams. Add another $275 million to her combined net worth and she'd be an official billionaire.

"Ma, your phone's ringing," Joselyn said from the armchair she was reclined in. "Looks like it's that Muslim woman."

Whitney gave a nod but kept the warming sun on her face a moment longer before she pivoted and walked to her spot on the sofa. The furniture was Italian, burgundy in color, and upholstered in some kind of velvety fabric that Whiteny hadn't researched before letting Joselyn charge it to her American Express Black card.

She sat down and picked up her ringing iPhone from the glass-top coffee table. The caller's identity was saved as Jamila, but that was the name she'd been given when she converted to Islam. Her birth name was Harmonique Evans. Whiteny stuck two AirPods in her ears before accepting the FaceTime call.

"Hey, beautiful," Jamila said.

"Hey, girl. Any good news?"

Jamila's pretty lips widened into a pretty smile. This was the first time Whitney had seen her without a cloth wrapped around her head to conceal her hair from the public.

"And where's your abaya?" Whitney added.

"Oh, fuck that abaya. All that religious bullshit is over for me. There was no Angel Gabriel who went into that cave and spoke with Allah's Holy Prophet. In fact, there is no Allah. No God, no Buddha - all of it's fake, created by mankind to keep the human population in line. How did God create the earth and the heavens ten thousand years ago when paleontologists are still studying million-year-old dinosaur fossils? What kind of God would let some killer with a green bandana tied around his face just run up and shoot my fiancé's head off right in front of me?" She waited, but only for a couple of seconds. "Exactly. Exactly. Man is evil. Plain and simple. And if there's a God up there watching over all this evil, then he's in on it."

Whitney snickered merrily at Jamila's theatrical tirade.

"And don't call me Jamila no more. I'm Harmonique. That's the name my mama gave me, that's who the fuck I am."

"Okay,"

Harmonique was a gray-eyed stunner with light brown skin and very full lips that made Whitney suspect there might have been a collagen injection or two in her past. Her face was shaped like an upside down egg, and it was beautiful. Not even the tirade could make Harmonique an ugly woman. A lustrous black long bob framed her gorgeous visage. The black leather headrest Whitney had glimpsed as Harmonique was swaying her head and raging at the gods had to be custom-designed, because it had snarling tiger clawing at Bentley's signature letter *B*.

"Girl," Whitney said, "Will you please calm down and get to the good news? If you're calling to tell me that Markio's in Michigan City, I already heard that. Nobody's *seen* him. I need to know where he's at."

Harmonique's pretty smile returned, and her eyebrows jumped twice. "You first," she said.

"Me first?" Whitney furrowed her brow. "I don't understand."

Across the room, Joselyn giggled at something she was watching on her iPhone. She had her AirPods in. her dark blue Chanel pajama pants were baggy, while her white-and-blue Chanel tee was skintight. She and her older sisters, identical twins Eva and Ava, had inherited their mother's small waist and big butt – the Clarrett girls, Whitney included, were so thick below the waist that their DNA could likely be traced back to the Khoisan tribes of southern Africa - but Joselyn was the only one who'd gotten her mama's big boobs.

"Go on," Harmonique said, regaining Whitney's attention. "I wanna know how much you settled for. I saw on *TMZ* that you and Alexus had settled out of court less than a month after you filed that lawsuit, and I know she's worth north of four hundred billion, so I wanna know how much she handed over for you to stop talkin' about what happened to you at the Versace Mansion."

"That is confidential information. I signed a non-disclosure agreement."

"Markio's location is also confidential, but I know where he's at. So tell me. How much did you get?"

$350 million, Whitney thought, *wired right to my checking account on the fifteenth of May.* What she said was, "Nine figures. Okay? You happy? Now tell me what you know."

Harmonique accepted the small victory with another hitch of the eyebrows. "He's at the Lighthouse Mall, shopping with a girl who's almost the spitting image of you. Long silky hair, high yellow complexion, slim waist, big butt. He definitely has a type. They're in the Gucci store. Hold on, I'll send you a video."

In the video, Markio and his female companion were perusing a rack of swimwear. Two fo Markio's older cousins - the skinny, pecan-brown Buck and the slightly shorter, much lighter head Kay - we're lingering nearby, trying on sunglasses.

The video was only four seconds long. Whitney watched it twice. By the end of the second viewing her nostrils were flared and her teeth were clenched.

"That bitch don't look like me," Whiteny said.

Harmonique snorted a chuckle. "I knew you was gon' say that. Listen: herb got a girl in three. She's with one of Markio's friends. All she's found out so far is that he's about to have some type of party with his family, but he'll be linking up with the boy Herb's girl is with later on tonight. That's when it'll happen."

"Who is the friend?"

For a moment Harmonique looked confused. Then her brow unwrinkled and she said, "Oh. You mean the guy with Herb's girl. I don't know his name. It might've been Moochie. Or Loochie. I know it rhymes with Gucci. I'll find out."

"No need." Whitney's sinister scowl became a conspiratorial smirk. She heard Joselyn giggle again, but this time she didn't look. "I know who it is."

Whitney knew just about everyone in her hometown.

"I'm gonna need some help paying for this," Harmonique said. "Just the old man. I don't think he's gonna pay his crew. He wants two million. I got one."

"Money's not an issue." And it wasn't just because of the money Whitney had gotten from Alexus Costilla-King.

Shortly before she was kidnapped, Whitney and her then-boyfriend Voltaire Much had invested in a Super Bowl commercial for her lip gloss and lipstick company, iKiss Kosmetics. That investment, combined with the intense media coverage of her kidnapping, had resulted in hundreds of millions of dollars in sales. She'd already had a net worth of $375 million even before she settled out of court with the world's wealthiest woman.

Whitney Clarrett was rich.

Even so, she still wanted Markio Earl dead. He'd fucked her out of two and a half million dollars at a time when she had nothing, left her for broke and moved on to the celebrity attorney who'd just given a statement on his behalf to a throng of news reporteres in front of MTN Towere, which was just a few blocks south of Whitney's Ontario Steet condo. When that relationship failed, Markio had fallen for Prinny Kelly, a reality TV show producer, and the shady motherfucker had then left Prinny for her supermodel half-sister, Kamari White. He became a New York Times bestselling novelist and the Oscar-nominated screenwriter of several movies, a celebrity in his own right, and he'd never even sent Whitney a text message to see if she and her children were alright.

Yeah, she definitely wanted him dead. And she'd visit the cemetery to piss on his grave when he was buried.

She ended the call with Harmonique and then phoned a man whose nickname had been Pudgy until Markio pulled a shotgun and blew off his left hand. Now Pudgy was called Nubby.

"I'm at work," said Nubby.

"Anybody else around you right now?"

"Nah. nope. But I ain't supposed to be on the phone."

"What year was that when Markio shot your hand off?"

There was a pause. When Nubby spoke again he sounded exasperated. Maybe even angry. "You tryna make fun of me or some'n?"

Whitney smiled without moving her lips. "Now you know I wouldn't do that. I'm just saying. You hate Markio just like I do. I know your sons are in the streets, just like you used to be. He's at the Lighthouse Mall right now, at the Gucci store. I got fifty thousand cash for you to walk off your bog right now, and another fifty if Markio doesn't make it out of that parking lot."

She sat back on the sofa, extended her legs, crossed them at the ankles, and giggled like Joselyn as she listened to Nubby quit his job in the loudest, most insolent way.

"Count your seconds, Markio," she muttered. "Count your motherfucking seconds."

Chapter 6

Morena pointed a forefinger at the two white diamond pendants that were lynched from Markio's duo of Cuban link necklaces. FREE LORD N'EM, read one. FBS VON, read the other. Her finger wagged from the first pendant to the second and back to the first again.

"Let me guess," she said. "All that's gang related."

Markio showed her his teeth and didn't say a thing. His silence spoke volumes. Rolling her eyes, Morena turned back to the mirror she'd been studying her reflection in and adjusted the new white bucket that Markio had just plopped on her head. It was the same color as the rather revealing one-piece bathing suit and strappy sandals he'd picked out for her a couple of minutes earlier.

His cousin Slime had arrived moments earlier with two other boys who called themselves Bee Baby and Bloody Boy. slime wore plain white low-top Air Force 1's, white deep-pocketed shorts with AMIRI printed across the hem of both knees, and a white tee that had Green Flag Activity emblazoned across the chest in slimy green lettering, like the cover of a *Goosebumps* book. Slime's dreads barely made it past his ears. VVS diamonds shone around his neck and wrists. His skin complexion was three shades browner than Markio and two lighter than Buck, like a cup of coffee with a tablespoon of milk stirred in. He was exactly six feet tall. His two friends wore the exact same tee-shirt he had on, and they too were iced out. They were all around the store, culling items from shelves, tables, and clothing racks.

There were three store clerks, a cashier, two security guys, and a store manager, all of them white, all of them watching. But none of them seemed particularly worried. Markio had lifted a fifty thousand dollar stack of hundreds from inside his white leather LV duffle and handed it to one of the store clerks as soon as he walked through the door, and that had put smiles on all of their faces. Kay, Buck, Slime, Bee Baby, and Bloody Boy all had their tall piles of hundreds in hand, cashing out the clerks as they selected more and more items from the store shelves.

"Brittany, Amanda, and I," Morena said, "We looked you up. There were a lot of articles about you. Some of them - how should I say this - they didn't paint you in the best light."

"What did you expect?" Markio shrugged and pushed out his bottom lip. "It's the Internet."

"Yeah, but a lot of it's true. One YouTube blogger was able to piece together a really plausible theory that you were a high-ranking member of the Traveling Vice Lords. He showed pictures of you with three or four other leaders of that gang. Your pendant says Free Lord N'em. I'm not slow, you know. I may be from Maryland, but I've been in the Midwest for half of my life. I know about the street gangs."

Another dismissive shrug from Millionaire Markio. He admired her fat round butt for the twentieth time this hour and then turned his head to look at Loochie and the young Haitian woman he'd walked in with ten or eleven minutes ago. She'd introduced herself as Regine Dorvilus. She was short, roughly the same height as Markio, and despite her heavy Caribbean accent, she spoke in the same Chicago street patois Mariko had grown up hearing and speaking in North Lawndale. She was brown like maple syrup, with a pie-shaped face that was reasonably attractive. Markio liked her because she had a big round butt - not nearly as big and round as Morena's, but a big butt was a big butt - and her radiant smile warmed the room.

There was an old-school Hip Hop song that warned against trusting a big butt and a smile, but what black man had ever been strong enough to resist that luscious combo of temptation?

Regine was testing a perfume on her inner wrist. Markio thought she looked vaguely familiar, but Regine told him that she'd grown up in Norwood Park, and he couldn't remember ever driving that far north. Not to the most segregated city in America. White neighborhoods like Lake View, Beverly, Mount Greenwood, Forest Glen, Norwood Park, and even Lincoln Park, where Markio's sprawling 25,000-square-foot mansion, the House of Lords, now stood, had always been off limits to black men from North Lawndale - or any black Chicago neighborhood, for that matter. Black men of his mien were often relegated to predominantly Black neighborhoods like Lawndale, Austin, Grand Crossing, New City, and Englewood, struggling communities where the frustrated denizens often used drugs and alcohol to soothe their financial aches, cracked sidewalks where the gangs run wild, death is cheap, and police harassment is inevitable.

When Markio took Morena's purchases to the front of the store to pay, he realized that he would be relinquishing a lot more than the fifty grand he'd placed in the hands of one nerdy-looking white girl. Shakia was at the encounter waiting - with a vast assortment of Gucci belts, shoes, shirts, fragrances, dresses, pants, hats, and shades piled high in front of her.

"You can ring all this up with whatever he's getting for her," Shakia said to the cashier. She glimpsed the few items Markio laid across the countertop for Morena and then looked at Morena like she was staring at a crazy woman. "Girl, you better quit playin'! Don't be coy. Go and getchoo three or four more of those swimsuits, three or four more of those hats. Some more sandals. Some shoes. A purse. Girl, come with me."

The cashier was also a younger white woman, a homely faux blonde with big ears and a small face. Her bronze name pin read Debbie. She giggled like a high school teen as she watched Shakia drag Morena off by the wrist. The sweet little laugh, and the gleeful smile that accompanied it, raised her level of attraction from below negative to four levels above it. She swiveled that merry smile onto Markio. "Women, right? We'll want to shop until *you* drop."

Markio laughed and lifted another big pile of hundred-dollar bills out of his Louis Vuitton duffle. "You can ring it all up. The girl in the white dress is my sister."

"Oh, I know. I follow you on Insta. You're Millionaire Markio. My boyfriend took me to see *The Bird Man*. the first one and the second one. We thought we'd be the only white people in there." - she giggled mirthfully - "But there were a bunch of us. You get a lot of support from people out here."

"It's my second home," he said, more proudly than intended. He was zipping his duffle shut when Regine came over and raised her inner wrist to his nose. "What do you think?"

The first thing Markio thought of was "What Did I Miss?" - a fairly new Drake song in which the Canadian rap star repeatedly leveled the question at the friends of his who'd switched up on him in the wake of his war of words with Kendrick Lamar.

The next thought, formulated as Markio sniffed Regine's wrist and stared into her almond-shaped eyes, was that he'd definitely seen her before. He just couldn't remember where.

He nodded twice. "Smells good." Regine lowered her arm, and Markio added, "You're beautiful, by the way. I like your smile. And your eyes."

Regine's gorgeous chocolate visage lit up like the eastern horizon at sunrise. Had she been lighter in complexion, she would have blushed.

"I know you from somewhere," Markio said.

The light in her face dimmed by a good two hundred watts. "No. I've never met you before. My parents would have strangled me if they ever heard I was hanging out in North Lawndale, and this is my first time ever visiting Indiana. I don't go to nightclubs. The only concerts I've ever been to were Erykah Badu, Jill Scott, and Beyonce. Plus, you know, I would've remembered it if we ever met."

"You sure?"

She nodded fast. "Maybe we saw each other in traffic or something. You saw me and I didn't see you. I don't know." She shrugged and Markio observed that her shoulders were firm with muscles. So was the six-pack she had showing below her yellow crop top. "Is it cool if I come to your party? I can link back up with Loochie later."

Markio shook his head no and hated himself for doing it. "It's a family affair. I'm definitely slidin' on Loochie, though. Just be patient. You'll see me."

"Can I get a selfie?"

As Markio cozied up next to Regine for the picture, he glanced at the glistening diamonds in her necklace and wristwatch. They weren't much different from the jewelry Markio had on. Who was this mystery woman? Whoever she was, it was clear that she had some money. A diamond Chanel watch didn't come cheap, and Markio knew that the three blingy Tiffany bracelets on her other wrist had set someone back a teeth-clenching amount.

One of the clerks directed Regine to a second register, where she paid for the seven or eight items in her bag with a stack of hundreds and fifties she took from her purse. Then she and Loochie left the store, and Markio stared after her in a kind of thoughtful wonderment, trying hard to remember where he'd seen her in the past. He didn't think he'd ever heard her voice, but the way she walked, the way she looked - he was almost a hundred percent certain he'd seen that before. Somewhere.

Shakia loaded up four more shopping bags for Morena. The total bill came up to $78, 422.98. When Markio told the long-eared cashier that she and her coworkers could split the twenty-one thousand and change, she teared up, rubbed her distended belly, and either moaned or sighed or sobbed, or maybe she did all three simultaneously. Markio didn't realize that Debbie was pregnant, and showing until that very moment.

He and his entourage left the store at exactly two o'clock.

Chapter 7

The Altima that Nubby and his oldest son were in was brown and shiny like cold, congealed gravy. Julius had taken the rear license plate off and tossed it on the backseat.

They were parked near the corner of 8th Street and Ohio Street, just across the road from the Lighthouse Mall's fenced-in parking lot. A lot of the white-lined parking slots were filled, but Nubby had no trouble making out the two wide Rolls-Royces that were parked close to the mall. He couldn't miss them even if he tried. People kept raising their smartphones to snap photos of the two gaudy vehicles as they walked and drove past.

"We need to rob this nigga first," said Julius.

He was brown-skinned like his pops but lighter around the nose, as if an alien spacecraft had dropped down from the heavens and left a crop circle in the middle of his face. His head was a thimble with a swirled caramel coating of skin. He was thirty-one, twenty-one, twenty years his father's junior, and he was much tougher than his old man. Much more aggressive. His stout fingers strangled the butt of his Glock pistol.

"Nigga, you crazy," Nubby said. "The bitch says she wants this man dead. That's what we *came* to do, that's what we *gon'* do. Don't go gettin' no stupid-ass ideas."

"We need to rob him first," Julius repeated. "That lil thirty thousand dollars me and you splittin' ain't got shit on what he got in his pocket. I guarantee you that. He done made a hun'ed million dollars in the last year alone, all off books and movies. Saw that on *Forbes*. You can Google it."

Nubby, whose given name was Julius Troy Tucker Sr., was shaking his bald head the entire time. "She said leave him right here in this parkin' lot. We gon' catch him right there and –"

"Pops, you know that mall got a hun'ed cameras."

"That's why we gon' catch him pullin' *out*. That way we can just pull up next to him. You hang out and bang out, and we'll be thirty grand to the good."

Julius thrust his lower lip forward and said nothing, choosing to let his heavy nasal exhalation speak for him. This was about more than the money they stood to gain from Whitney Clarrett. This was about the left hand Nubby lost twenty years ago. That hard truth lay prone beneath the murder-for-hire plot like a red-eyed boogeyman under a four-year-old's bed. Nubby knew it and Julius knew it, though neither man said it.

They both wore jeans and dark-colored tees. There hadn't been time to grab any masks or gloves. Julius had been laid up with his latest new trophy, a petite young White babe, when Nubby stopped by to pick him up in his two-year-old Chevy pickup. He'd lift his truck there. The Altima belonged to the babe.

"Light me a square," Nubby said, meaning cigarette.

Julius was lifting the pack of Newports from the center console when Nubby grabbed his wrist.

"Look. That's him. That's his bitch-ass right there." Nubby pointed his nub straight ahead.

Six men had just emerged from between two low buildings, with two happy women leading the way. Nearly all of them carried shopping bags. The woman in the purple tee shirt and jeans was the only one who didn't have a bunch of diamonds glimmering around her neck and wrists. Utilizing his iPhone high-definition zoom feature, Nubby zoomed in on the menagerie of departing shoppers and got a close-up look at the man who'd pulled a 12-gauge shotgun from inside his baggy sweatpants and blasted a slug through Nubby's lower left forearm.

That was twenty whole years ago, but Nubby remembered it like it was yesterday.

He had just moved his family from Fort Wayne to Michigan City, his wife Erica Lender's hometown. A lifelong trapper, he'd set up shop in a crackhead's ramshackle home on East 10th Street, right up the street from where a clique of wild young dope boys who called themselves the Tenth Street Hustlers got their money. None of them had ever complained about the newcomer. There was more than enough cash to go around. All day long and through the night, drug addicts had cruised East 10th Street with cash in hand, hungry for crack rocks. Back then it was nothing for Pudgy (as he was called at the time) to get rid of two whole ounces in a single day and drive home about four thousand dollars richer.

But then one of the Tenth Street Hustlers had made the ignorant and very dangerous mistake of shooting some Chicago nigga for knocking him out at a dice game. The following night, two dark vehicles - a Dodge Intrepid and a minivan - had pulled up to where a crowd was gathered near the corner of 10th and Lafayette, and someone rose up out of the Intrepid and opened fire on the entire crowd.

A pretty teenage girl called Neek Neek was shot. The dozen or so others who ran, jumped fences, and ducked low next to curbside sedans had survived the hail of gunfire without so much as a graze, but those shooting survivors were still scarred. The Tenth Street Hustlers stopped hustling. At least on 10th Street they did. All but the most desperate drug addicts dared to venture through that area. Pudgy was lucky if he made eighty dollars in a day.

Frustrated, he'd driven his candy-painted Cadillac sedan to the city's west side, to find Markio, the rowdy young Chicagoan everyone was blaming for the 10th Street shooting. Pudgy found him on Willard Avenue, in the mouth of an alleyway between 7th and 8th streets. He and another teen boy were standing next to the redbrick building that had then housed a liquor store. Markio was handing something small enough to go unseen to a fortyish Black woman with wild hair and no fat on her bones, and she in turn was handing him a bunch of crinkled dollar bills.

Markio stopped counting the dollars and stuffed them in the side pocket of his tan-colored sweatpants when Pudgy turned into the alleyway. He reached down into his sweatpants and bent forward to peer into the Cadillac.

"Ay, is you Markio?" Pudgy had asked with his left arm hanging out over his door.

"Why?"

"Because, nigga, I can't get no mothafuckin money down there on 10th Street 'cause you done scared all the goddam clientele off. You need to calm that shit down! How the fuck I'm s'pose to feed my -"

There was a flash of chrome as the single-barreled shotgun came out of Markio's sweatpants, then a hellacious bloom of fire that compelled Pudgy to slam his Jordan shoe down on the gas pedal. His Cadillac was halfway down the alleyway when he brought his arm in and saw that his hand and wrist were hanging on by just a few ragged shreds of bloody flesh. The surgical doctors at St. Anthony couldn't save it. Too much damage, they'd said. Detectives from the Michigan City Police Department had shown him five lineups of potential suspects, three of which had mugshots of the man who'd shot him, but he hadn't snitched. He wasn't raised to be a rat. He'd done four years in federal prison when he and his Fort Wayne crew were indicted for drug trafficking. He hadn't snitched on them, and he hadn't snitched on Markio.

Now though, as he sat in the driver's seat of the gravy-brown Altima, watching Millionaire Markio gaze wantonly at the glorious backside of a beautiful young woman with an

Alicia Keys complexion and Kardashian curves, Nubby found himself wishing he'd told those MCPD detectives everything he knew. It was a spiteful thought, he chastised himself for even thinking it, but it was there just the same.

A muscle in the right side of his top lip ticked upward and stayed that way. Unconsciously, he flexed all the muscles in his left arm, from the shoulder all the way down to the stump. He was still wearing the dark green shirt and black jeans he'd worn to his shitty call center gig, and though the Altima's cool air was blowing just fine, a sudden heatwave swept through him. It started somewhere in the salt-and-pepper stubble atop his nearly bald head and worked its way down from there.

He and Julius watched Markio on the iPhone screen until he and the two girls disappeared from view beside a parked SUV. The trunk of the first Phantom popped open, and Nubby got a glimpse of Markio through the SUVs window. It seemed he was loading shopping bags into the trunk.

"Bitch-ass nigga," Nubby muttered, sounding like a bitch-ass nigga.

"We got eeeem." Julius sounded excited. His crop circle face was one big smile. "I ain't gon' lie, I need that fifteen racks. Shit, I would'a did it for ten."

Why didn't I offer the nigga ten thousand? Nubby thought as he rotated the key and got the engine chugging. *Could've kept ninety to myself.*

A petty thought from a petty man.

Chapter 8

Morena's pale-lipped smile was as warm and endearing as a romantic ballad performed by the great Jennifer Hudson.

"Thank you so, so, *so* much," she said, beaming sweet rays of joy. "Nobody's ever taken me shopping like this. Oh my God, thank you so much. I love you already. Whatever you're trying to d o to me, it's working."

She shrieked and did a joyful little jump. Markio was putting the shopping bags in the trunk of his Phantom, but he paused long enough to see what that jump did to Morena's fat round bottom. The resulting jiggle made him shake his head in raw amazement. He sandwiched his bottom lip between his teeth and bit down hard.

Morena had a new purple tote bag, only this one had Gucci's signature double G logo imprinted all over it. She squatted low on her haunches and began transferring things from the old tote to the new one.

"Wait until I show all this to Brittany. She is going to lose it." She looked over and up at Markio. Her sexy eyes were shaded by a purple bucket hat. He'd bought her that same hat in four different colors. "You know, she's the one who dug up all the dirt on you. The murder conviction. That shady affair you had with Karmari White, your ex Prinny Kelly's half-sister. She even showed me a selfie video of Kamari talking about how good you were in bed, the one where Kamari says you got *superdick*." With a soft, buttery giggle, Morena threw a glance at the front of Markio's off-white LV

SUPER GREMLIN 5 | KING RIO

shorts and then returned her gaze to his face. "Any truth to that?"

"You gon' find out reeeal soon," he said.

She snickered for a long time at that.

Slime walked over. "Ay, five," he said, picking up the last couple of shopping bags and wedging them in the trunk, "I'ma need you before I shoot back down to Louisiana. You already know what it is, five. What I'm on."

Markio gave a nod. One thing he liked about Slime was that he never beat around the bush. He also had a pretty good idea of what Slime needed from him.

"We'll talk about it at the party," Markio said.

Slime rubbed the side of his neck and twisted his head from left to right, grimacing as he did it. When his hand came down it revealed a blue-black bruise that looked like the splayed bristles of a narrow paintbrush. Markio hadn't noticed it before, because Slime was wearing five thick Cuban-links.

"What the fuck happened to yo' neck?"

"Big nigga tried to snatch my chain at the club back home, ya heard me? He caught me walkin' to the restroom and yanked my shit. You know we had to buss his head. It's North Side, Thirty-eighth, we put guns to da face, ya heard me?"

Whenever Slime said ya heard me, it wasn't because he thought the listener might be in need of a hearing aid. It was the Louisiana way of saying ya feel me.

Markio grinned at the knowledge that his cousin's attacker had been put away in gangster fashion. Morena gave him a look but she didn't say anything. She tossed her emptied tote bag into the closing trunk, shouldered the costly new Gucci tote, and sauntered around to her door, which Shakia had already opened.

"Always trickin' on some'n," Slime said. His lips parted in a southern grin that revealed twin rows of diamond encrusted teeth. A dimple appeared in his cheek.

The chuckle that tumbled forth from Markio's larynx was filled with a shameless guilt. He shook hands with the heroin-peddling killer whose birth name was Jarvon Barnett. It was a gang handshake that included signs for the Almighty Blood Nation and the Almighty Vice Lord Nation. After that Markio joined Morena in the backseat of his Phantom, while Slime went to the swampy green Mercedes Maybach SUV he'd had sitting in O'Hare's long-term parking section for the past several months.

"He sounds like NBA Youngboy," Morena said when their doors were shut. "You know who I'm talkin' about? That rapper?"

"They're from the same block. Grew up together."

"How do you know him?" "Who, Slime? That's my cousin. On my mama's side. Granny and Granddaddy brought my mama and all her sisters and brothers to Chicago from Baton Rouge over sixty years ago. We still got family down there."

"Did they leave during The Great Migration?"

Markio offered an awkward shrug. He was leaning forward, shifting his duffle bag around between his designer sneakers.

"Way before my time," he said. "All I know is that some white man called my grandmama a nigga, and my granddaddy shot him in the head. After that they left for Chicago."

"Hm. Wild." or maybe the word was *Wow*; Markio couldn't tell.

He sat back, watching the scenery in front of them change as Shakia backed out of the parking slot. Consciously, he was thinking about the bricks of heroin Slime had come to buy, and imagining the big fellow who'd made the very foolish mistake of trying to snatch a gangsta's chain. Subconsciously, he was on high alert, scanning the parking lot for any signs of the Grinch-faced sniper. Had Herb learned that he was laying low in Michigan City? Maybe the murderous old fuck had gotten it out of FBS Longshot before or after he shot the boy with a short gun.

Markio eyed an obese White woman and her skinny Black boyfriend as they climbed out of their Jeep and went walking off toward the mall. Three young Black women who were all reaching for the door handles on their pastel blue Honda Accord dropped their hands and stared at the passing Rolls-Royces. Outside the fence, a grayish white school bus with FAIRHAVEN BAPTIST CHURCH stenciled on the side in large burgundy letters went trundling east down 8th street, regaining the momentum it had lost as it slowed to cross the train tracks thirty feet back. A strawberry red Camaro with the top down streaked past going in the opposite direction, hardly braking at all before bumping over the tracks and continuing west. Shiny chrome rims that were at least thirty inches in diameter added a rich flare to the clean red convertible. The driver was a light-skinned young Black man with one hand clutching the wheel, like Jay-Z in that "Song Cry" video. His passenger was a young Black woman with darker skin and braided hair.

"Mind if I put us both in this selfie video for my Instagram Stories?" Morena was already raising her iPhone, poising her pouty pink lips like a seasoned supermodel.

Markio answered the question by leaning in with a grin on his face and holding up his thumb and first two fingers for the camera, the V and the L that symbolized Vice Lord.

Morena's eyes rolled but her mouth smiled.

Maybe it was the materialistic vanity that all the music, movies, and magazines had drilled into his psyche since he was a child, but Mariko thought Morena looked even sexier with the Gucci bucket hat on her head and the matching tote bag next to her hip. All she needed now was a nice diamond watch to complete the look.

He was thinking of the Audemars Piguet Royal Oak he'd gotten Mya, his son's mother, for Mother's Day this year, and Shakia was nearing the open section of chainlink fencing that would put them right out onto 8th Street, when a glint of sunlight reflected off the windshield of a Nissan sedan that was rolling towards them from Ohio Street, at the opposite side of 8th.

Markio froze in his seat. He kept his eyes on the Nissan. It was the color of nothing you'd remember.

The Nissan crept forward to the corner where Ohio intersected with 8th Street. Markio squinted. He could see two peanut butter pears in the windshield, moving toward his Phantom in a car that was a rolling shade of mute.

Morena was still filming content for her social media viewers, posing and vibing to the Ice Spice song Shakia had just turned on. The music was loud, but Markio hardly even heard it. Morena said her ex was going to be sooo jealous, but the statement didn't register in Markio's brain.

He glanced at the electronic control panel and pressed the touchscreen button that slid open the window, just as Shakia was braking at the gate to let a westbound ice cream truck jingle past.

As soon as the colorful truck was between Markio's black hooded white Rolls-Royce and the nothing colored Nissan, Markio shoved open his door and popped out with his Glock in hand.

Chapter 9

The ice cream truck was like a bad omen.

Everything was looking good for Nubby and Julius before it appeared, but the instant it passed, Nubby sped lacrosse the street and blocked the Phantoms in, and Julius stuck half his body out the window to take aim.

That was when things went bad.

Really bad.

The woman in the driver's seat of the leading Phantom - a pretty woman who bore a striking resemblance to the man they were after - managed to duck low half a second before Julius opened fire. His .40 caliber pistol had been converted into a machine gun, and it had a 30-shot clip. An enfilade of tenor fifteen copper bullets struck the Phantom's windshield, flattened, and bounced back onto the matte black hood, as if the windshield was made of some kind of next generation Gorilla Glass.

At the same time, Markio rose up from beside the Phantoms holding a Glock that looked like a replica of the one Julius was firing, only his wasn't a machine gun, and it didn't have an extended magazine down under the handle like a forlorn willow tree branch.

It was obvious that Markio was a skilled shooter. He held his Glock in both hands and walked forward as he pulled on the trigger. Three quick shots, and Julius made a sound like aman in the rapturous throes of orgasm. Two gruff grunts and a groan.

Nubby reached over and snatched his oldest boy back into the car, knowing Julius was hit but too focused on their getaway to take a look. You'd have thought he saw a poisonous spider crawling on the gas pedal the way he stomped down on it. He felt a bullet whiz past his chin, and another one blasted through his thumbnail, and then he was off like a rocket, lancing up 8th Street at a greatly increasing rate of speed, steering with his nub and squeezing what remained of his thumb in a very tight fist.

Julius grunted and coughed. Blood sprayed from his mouth, dotting the dashboard and windshield. A single droplet spotted the chin of a yellow Labubu doll someone had hung from the rearview mirror.

Nubby winced and drove on.

He made a hard right onto Washington Street, swerved around a black BMW coupe with a bespectacled young Latina sitting behind the wheel, and two blocks down he made a screeching left onto 10th Street, narrowly missing a middle-aged Black woman in a denim minidress who was walking across the street.

"You dumb bitch!" The woman screamed.

Nubby paid her no mind.

He slowed the car just long enough to assess his son's injuries and quickly looked away. Julius was shot at least once. There was an ugly red hole at the base of his throat. Dark blood bubbled out of it and sluiced down the chest of his navy blue Pacers tee. He grunted and gurgled and grabbed at his neck, then reached out and touched everything around him. The dashboard, the door panel, the ceiling, the center console. Bloody handprints galore.

"Shit!" Nubby exclaimed. "Shit motherfuckin' *shit!*" He gritted his teeth and grimaced, glanced at his throbbing, stinging, dripping fist, and drove on.

Chapter 10

"What are you in here cooking?"

"Carolina Gold Rice Midlands with Shrimp and Red Snapper." The name of the delectable Southern dish rolled off Whiteny's tongue like a raindrop off a leaf. "And I used the shrimp shells to make the stock, it'll be good. Trust me. It'll be more than good. If this ain't the best seafood dish you've ever had in your life, I'll suck your dick until my jaws ache."

She smiled at the handsome grin she saw from the corner of her eye.

Almost three hours had passed since she got off the phone with Nubby. Her youngest daughter had left to hang out with a fellow social media influencer and her youngest glover had just arrived.

He was twenty-one years old, and his name was Aaron Michael Meadows. Everyone called him Flocka, like the rapper, though the two men looked nothing alike besides the fact that they both wore their hair in dreadlocks. This Flocka had a much darker complexion, and his build was way more muscular. He was six feet five now, two hundred and fifty pounds of rock hard muscle. Their love was a scandalous affair, as he was her son Jimmy's best friend and, most scandalous of all, her daughter Ava had been his girlfriend for almost three years.

Flocka smacked her on the right buttock and squeezed the round mound of fat she had back there. He kissed her once on the ball of her shoulder, then again on the side of her neck.

She was busy with her long wooden spoon, stirring diced shallots, celery, and onions into a thin layer of olive oil, but she wasn't too busy to turn her head and suck lips with a man-child who was almost eighteen years younger than she was.

She didn't think she'd ever be too busy for that.

The passionate kiss lasted a good twelve seconds. When their wet lips finally parted, Whitney was almost panting, and the front of Flocka's blue Givenchy cargo shorts was sticking straight out like a tepee. His broad chest swelled and retracted at a respiratory pace that bordered on hyperventilation. His white-and-blue tee was as tight on him as Whitney's dress was on her. On his right wrist he wore the rose gold rolex Sky Dweller that Whitney had gifted him on Juneteenth.

"Fuck that food, baby," he said, moving to stand behind her. He lowered his chin into the crook of her neck, put his strong dark hands on her wide hips, and pressed his erection against her ass. "You got all day to cook. Just lemme get twenty minutes. I swear, that's all I need."

"No, boy." Whitney giggled and shook her head. "I gotta make my risotto." She went on stirring. "There's actually a story to the rice grits you use for this recipe. Rice grits were the broken grains that were used to feed enslaved Africans. Because it was so cheap, you know. None of the Whites wanted broken grains, so it was used for the slaves."

She picked up a white porcelain bowl of Carolina Gold rice grits, dumped it into the pan, and mixed it in, adding a dash of salt and a spoon of tomato pasta to the risotto, then half a cup of saffron, and then deglazing the whole mixture with a bit of white wine before ladling in the shrimp stock.

"It do smell good," Flocka opined.

"Yes. it does." Whitney shut her eyes and inhaled through her nose. "So good. Eva always asks me to cook this. It's been her favorite meal ever since she was eight. She'll kill me if I don't save her a plate."

"You heard what happened to Markio?"

Feigning ignorance, Whitney shook her head. "No. What happened?"

"They say some niggas caught him leaving he Lighhouse Mall out there in Michigan City and shot up his Rolls-Royce. I heard it from Tonya, Kela, and Bambi. They were right there in the parking lot when the whole shit went down."

"Was he shot?"

Flocka shook his chin on her shoulder. His dick was still a throbbing length of desire on her butt.

"I don't think so. He hopped out and shot back. Shot the nigga who was tryna shoot him. Tonya got a cousin work at St. Anthony's. She said two Fort Wayne niggas showed up at the hospital all shot up. Father and son, both named Julius Tucker. Say the son got it worse. He got shot twice in the chest and once in the neck. Died before they could even get him on the operating table."

A contemplative silence ensued. Whitney turned off the stove and put a lid over the deep pan. She considered asking Flocka to go after Markio. She'd done it before, shortly after Markio had fucked her out f the two-point-five million dollars in cash that was rightfully hers. She'd had Flocka and one of his fellow Gangster Disciples break into a house that Markio was renting and search around for the cash-filled stainless steel suitcases she and Markio had gotten out of the locker they'd purchased at a storage auction. Sure, the thousand dollars that paid for the locker was Markio's but he never would have known about the auction if she hadn't told him about it. She'd signed *her* name on the papers to purchase the contents of that locker, because at the time she was his girlfriend, and she'd loved him with all her heart. He had found those suitcases loaded with more than five million dollars, and yet he'd only given her fifty grand, a lousy one percent of the loot. So yeah, she'd paid Flocka to do the break-in, and then she'd paid him to plant a tracking device on Markio's nephew Tyquan's vehicle, so that Voltaire muck and his posse of Zoe Pound gremlins could invade the rural farmhouse where Markio stashed all his drug shipments. All those missing kilos had ultimately led to Flocka being shot, Voltaire being killed, and Whitney being kidnapped, tortured, and starved for months and months on end.

A couple of years had passed since then. Flocka was infatuated with Whitney, but now there was no way she could get him to go against Markio. Flocka was rich because of Markio, rich beyond his wildest dreams. He'd moved back to his hometown, a southern Indiana city called Evansville. Every month or so, a box truck, usually driven by an innocent-looking White girl, would pull up behind Flocka's quarter-million-dollar home, and he and his younger cousin, Benji, would unload exactly nine cardboard boxes. Every load was the same: thirty pounds of exotic bud, five thousand pills, sixty pints of Wockhardt promethazine with codeine syrup, three bricks of heroin, ten bricks of fentanyl, and ten bricks of cocaine. Those drug loads had made Flocka a lot of money, which he'd used to finance the construction costs of Muscle Up, the private, members-only gym he'd opened in Geist, Indiana, a wealthy suburban town just outside of Indianapolis.

"Don't make me rape you in this kitchen," he said, and kissed her on the ear.

To most women who'd been kidnapped and raped in the past, such a statement might have caused them to dry right up. To Whitney Clarrett, however, the threat had the opposite effect. Those hungrily muttered words, combined with the firm grip of Flocka's powerful hands on her hips and the feel of his steel erection poking her in the butt, made her body heat up and her nipples harden.

She turned around to face him. Thought about untying the tan and brown checkered Louis Vuitton apron she'd put on to keep the food from splashing onto her dress and decided against it. Rested her forearms on his shoulders and gently caressed the nape of his neck with her fingertips while he looked down into her eyes and rubbed the palms of his hands up and down the generous swells of her butt.

"They say Black women only get better with age," Flocka said. He sucked in his bottom lip before adding, "That might be the biggest truth ever told."

"Boy, I'm so wet right now I could put out a fire."

"Good. My tongue on fire."

Whitney's eyes got big. Really big. The prospect of getting some head had always excited her. There was nothing like a man with a long, thick, talented tongue to get her juices flowing.

She took Flocka by the hand and preceded him out of the kitchen, a huge room with white marble countertops, white marble tiles for flooring, cream walls, and rosewood cabinetry. The fridge and stove were hulking stainless steel appliances, as were the toaster, blender, microwave, and block of knives that decorated the counter.

The kitchen was huge because the condo was huge. Over eight thousand square feet, spread out across two floors of dazzling white marble, brass, and glass. Six bedrooms, six baths, a Jacuzzi, a room with every product iKiss Kosmetics had ever released stacked on glass shelves along the walls. It was a thirty-two-million-dollar condo that Whitney was leasing for $45, 000-per-month.

One of the upstairs bedrooms had been converted into what could only be called a sex room. It was the room on the left at the far end of the east wing hallway, just across from the personal hair and nail salon where Whitney and her daughters sat down to get beautified twice or thrice a week.

Ascending the glass butterfly staircase with Flock in tow, Whitney took a long moment to ruminate over Nubby's failure to send Millionaire Markio on a one-way flight to heaven.

What the hell was I thinking, sending that dumb fuck to kill the same man who blew half his arm off twenty years ago? I should have called Pimp, or Timmy Louis, or maybe

Loochie. One of those Gary niggas who grew up killing people. Hell, I could have gone right to one of these Chicago neighborhoods and found some gangbanger who'd do it for five or ten grand.

A kiss on her rump brought her back to the present.

"You got the most perfect body I ever seen." Flocka delivered another loud, smacky kiss to her right butt cheek. "On gang, you the baddest woman I ever had in my life. No disrespect to Ava. She bad too, you know. But she ain't got shit on you."

As fucked up as the compliment sounded, Whitney couldn't repress the radiant smile that formed on her face.

The sex room door was hewn from a heavy slab of Honduran mahogany and painted cherry red. Inside, the carpet was a slightly darker red, and the ceiling and all four walls were covered in mirrors. Tall red standing lamps emitted a red glow of light that reached every corner of the room. There was a sex swing with a black leather seat. A long table draped in red cloth with a bunch of sex toys and lubricants neatly situated across it. An angular sofa-like contraption that allowed for all kinds of different sexual positions. A mirror-doored closet in one corner where Whitney stored a variety of sexy costumes and wigs.

"Get naked," Whitney ordered in the sharp, authoritative tone of a no-nonsense schoolteacher. "Shes, socks - everything."

Flocka was fully nude seven seconds later. So was Whitney. She rubbed him down in Johnson & Johnson baby oil and he did the same to her. She thought his dick was an inch or so longer than it was the first time she got a taste of it, back when he was eighteen and she was thirty-five. He'd always had an athletic build, but now his musculature was insane, like a dark brown balloon stuffed full of peanuts.

Whitney kissed him on the mouth, rising up on her flawlessly pedicured toes to do it. She went back down on the flats of her pretty feet and began pressing her lips against the glistening mesa of his right pectoral muscle, then switched over to the left one, all the while stroking and squeezing his fat black dick in both hands. She considered taking one or two pleasurable moments to smooch and rub the hard stacks of brown brick that made up his bodybuilder six-pack, but she was salivating much too heavily, much too *hungrily*, so she skipped over his abs and spat all her spit on his dick as she dropped down on her haunches.

There was an upward curvature to Flocka's erect phallus. The girth was more than impressive, and the length was either eight inches or very close to it. Whitney stroked her spit along its length and then sucked the fat head into her mouth. Getting her mouth around the first couple of inches was a struggle, but she managed. She established a steady rhythm of forth and back, applying the appropriate amount of suction and twisting her head from side to side and wishing his dick was thinner so she could get it to the back of her throat and choke on it.

"Oh shit," Flocka said.

"Mm hmm," Whitney hummed.

She'd learned that the clockwise and counterclockwise rotations of her head, combined with the appropriate amount of suction and an excessive amount of spit, was the key to making a man's knees spasm. No man had ever lasted more than five minutes in her mouth since she figured that out. The twist, the suck, and the spit. It was a combination that any woman could master.

"Oh *shit*," Flocka said again.

"Mm hmm," Whitney hummed again.

She massaged her swollen nipples between the thumb and forefinger of her left hand and cupped his heavy balls in her right hand. Two minutes passed, and she could feel the vaginal juices burgeoning within her. Three minutes passed, and Flocka's breathing became spasmodic. Another forty seconds passed and he tried to pull back but she grabbed him by the butt, forcing her head forward and lashing his cockhead with her tongue.

Flocka lasted another three seconds after that. Then he made a sound like a cowboy spurring his stallion forward – "Yahh!" – and shot a warm, thick load of cum into Whiteny's mouth. She dragged her wet lips back so that she was only sucking on the head and took his dick in both hands to jerk and squeeze the rest of it out of him, looking up at his fluttering eyelids as she did it.

She might have laughed if there wasn't so much salty ejaculate spewing out over her tongue and pooling in the back of her throat.

Flocka's knees buckled and trembled during those last few seconds of ecstasy. Deep, shaky breath blew in and out of his flared nose. A low sibilant noise escaped from between his clenched teeth.

When the spasms finally subside, Flocka looked down at Whitney with a grin of total relief brightening his annoyingly handsome visage. He chuckled once, paused, chuckled again. She popped her lips off the head of his dick, showed him the huge mess he'd made in her mouth, then closed her lips and swallowed before opening up to show him that all of his cum had bone down her throat.

That was the fourth and final step to a perfectly executed blow job. The swallow. Whitney didn't particularly care for that last step – especially when the semen was as slimy and plentiful as Flocka's – but it was an important step. Nasty but necessary. Like the little caps of NyQuil her parents used to give her when she was sick as a child.

The seminal aftertaste was so bitter in her throat that she halfway grimaced as she rose to her feet. Flocka smacked her on the ass and squeezed. She swallowed again, chasing the cumshot with spit.

"You the truth," he said, his broad chest rising and falling.

"Yeah, yeah, yeah. It's your turn now, nigga." Whitney went to the sex swing and mounted the seat. "Get on over here. Mama ain't got all day."

Flocka got down on his knees and walked to her that way, so that he resembled a man with severed legs. A man with nubs for legs. Which reminded Whitney of Nubby.

"The guys who shot at Markio," she said as she folded her legs back and used her fingertips to give her rigid clitoris a circular rub.

"What about 'em?" Flocka rubbed his big hands from her hips to the back of her knees.

"You said they both were shot, right?"

"Mm hm. Think she said the daddy only got shot once, though. Bullet blew the top of his thumb off. Which wouldn't be that bad if the nigga wasn't already missin' his other hand." He thumbed the hood of her clitoris back and gave it a gentle lick. "It's all bad for Daddy Tucker."

He snickered at his own humor and began flicking and twirling his tongue on Whiteny's most sensitive erogenous zone. Her eyes rolled forty degrees upward, her long lashes jittered, and she sucked in a breath that sounded like three separate inhalations done in rapid succession.

Whitney forgot all about Daddy Tucker and his obliterated limbs. She forgot about his dead son, too. When Flocka went low and dug his fat tongue into her tightly puckered ass hole, she might have even forgotten her name and date of birth.

Chapter 11

The murder weapon was registered in Shakia's name, which wasn't a problem, but Markio had done the shooting, which *was* a problem. A fairly big one when you look into account the Michigan City Police Department's years-long vendetta against him.

He'd called his attorney, Nikkia Staples, as soon as he got back to the beach house. She told him to stay on the property, and to keep quiet about the shooting, two suggestions he would have followed anyway. Since that call she'd been texting him every thirty minutes. No arrest warrant had yet to be issued, but she was almost certain that one was on the way. So was he. After all, the shooting had taken place in the parking lot entrance of a shopping mall. Too many cameras. Too many eyewitnesses.

"First date and you almost got my best friend murdered. The fuck is up with that?"

Markio looked up from his phone with a smirk on his face and a smile in his mien. It was the foul-mouthed blonde with the pretty blue eyes. Brittany Long.

He'd cancelled the yacht party and was instead holding it inside the beach house,in the glass-ceilinged room where an in-ground swimming pool was the centerpiece to a 2, 000-square-foot rectangle of living space that included a nightclub-style bar, an eighteen-person Jacuzzi, a mechanical bull, and a section of aqua blue sofas and glass-top tables for those who preferred a more comfortable vibe.

Markio was one of the latter.

"I ain't did shit," he said.

"Bullshit you didn't do shit," Brittany said, planting her delicate little ivory hands on her very narrow hips. She was wearing a white string bikini, and her long hair was tired back in a swirling topknot. "She won't tell me what it is you did, but she also won't tell me what it is you didn't do, and that pretty much tells me everything."

"Yeah?" Markio's smirk grew an inch on both sides. He sat back on the sofa, folded his arms over his chest.

"Yeah. She tells me everything. *Every*thing."

"How did you even know where I live?"

"Because I'm top flight security of the world, Craig. I don't play about my friends. We share locations. She was supposed to text me, and when she didn't, I showed up."

"In a string bikini," Markio noted.

"Yup." An electric smile shocked her stone-hard features to life. "I'll take it right off and strangle you with it." She nodded her head in agreement with her own threat, a jerky little nod that made her topknot bob like a small boat in a big ocean. "We read all about how you had your goons snatch Whitney Clarrett from outside that strip club. That's why the feds raided your house out there in Chicago. Probably why you're hiding out here in this small-ass town. Or is it the eighty-year-old elite military sniper who's after you? Huh? Which is it?"

"The elite military sniper."

Brittany's smile went so wide that Markio was certain a laugh would follow. But it didn't. Her big blue eyes flicked upward to the low waves on his head and then scanned him all the way down to his shoes. Her smile had expanded a little more by the time her eyes made it back to his face.

"That truck you got," he said. "Did you get it in silver for a reason?"

Brittany's question mark came in the form of a furrowed brow.

"Tellurium," he said. "That chemical element. That's what Telluride means. It's silverish-white. They use it in semiconductors."

She raised and lowered her pinkish-white right shoulder. "I didn't even know that. My dad actually brought it. He got tired of seeing me riding around in that beat-to-shit Sportage. I'd have to …"

She trailed off and swiveled the upper half of her body to look back over her shoulder. That was because Morena had just started screaming.

The swimming pool was roughly twenty feet behind the bikini-clad blonde. Just about everyone was in it, and Morena was shooting down the twenty-foot water slide with her hands in the air and her mouth wide open.

"Okay, I have to try that. I *have* to try that," Brittany said, and she ran off towards the slide like an overly excited child on her first trip to Disneyland.

Markio watched the jiggle of her small round derriere until she was a good twenty feet away. He couldn't help it. A round ass on a woman was a round ass on a woman, no matter how fat it was.

Fifteen years in prison had given him a staunch appreciation of the female gender.

He went back to surfing the web on his iPhone, going from news site to news site. Focusing on the news was a struggle. He kept thinking of Pudgy, wondering how he and his son (the passenger had to be his son, he looked just like Pudgy) had known to come to the lighthouse Mall. someone had to have told them. Markio had driven to the Dairy Queen and then to the mall with his curtains closed. It was possible that Pudgy and Twanika Marsh were associates, maybe through social media, but Nika didn't know that Markio's two Rolls-Royces had gone to the mall after he signed her book. Morena and the Haitian girl were the only people who'd captured video of him at the mall, and both of them were new to town.

At least he thought they were.

Meeting Morena at Washington Park beach was a chance encounter, initiated by an expensive French bulldog with a bottomless appetite. But what about Regine? Why had she been so pressed to meet Markio in the first place? Sure, he had his share of crazed superfans, but Regine hadn't given off that vibe. She'd been happy to meet him, but not too happy. Not superfan happy. On top of that, she'd been wearing the kind of jewelry Markio bought for the women in his life, real ice that had cost someone, or maybe a few someones upwards of six figures.

He was thinking about those diamonds and their origins when he heard Brittany go shrieking down the water slide. He looked up from his phone screen. Amanda Stanley was the first person his eyes landed on. she was standing poolside, jumping up and down and laughing as her cousin went rocketing into the water. Amanda was a small woman, a very small woman with very pretty features. Markio thought she might be four and a half feet tall. A sexy little blond elf who might tempt Santa into creeping around on Mrs. Claus.

They weren't the only Whites in the room. The yacht crew consisted of five women and five men, and all but two of them were White. Markio had paid the captain thirty grand for a twelve-hour shift, and since he had moved the yacht party into the beach house, the yacht crew had joined the indoor festivities. They were all over the room. One managed the mechanical bull while another made sure no one lost their footing on the water slide ladder. One fixed drinks behind the bar and another carried drinks around on a gold-plated tray, offering them to the guests. One was a chef, another a chef's assistant, and a third was the waitress who wrote down orders on a pocket-size notepad and took them out to the kitchen. A nubile young Black woman worked the floor in a white frilled knee-length skirt and white pole shirt, cleaning up after guests and drying the floor in places and smiling like she was preparing to be photographed for a school yearbook. That smile blazed with real happiness. Markio spent a long moment watching it before he turned his head to scan the rest of the room.

His sister Shakia and her girlfriend Shanese were in attendance. So was his sister Mariah, her husband Justin, and her two besties, Jesseca and Shavonne. Huey – Kay and Buck's older brother – was in the pool with his wife, Dee Dee. Buck and his wife, Lana, were also in the water, while Kay and his girlfriend, JoJo, were at the bar with Tito, Huey and Dee Dee's son. The rest of the family was either in line for a bull ride, gathered poolside in boisterous conversation, or seated around the cloth-covered square tables behind the sofa that was directly across from the one Markio was seated on. They were laying spades at two of those tables. The eight men surrounding a third table were shaking dice in their own peculiar styles and rolling them across the table for large amounts of cash. Three of them were Slime and his Bloods and the other five rocked dazzling chains with icy FBS pendants. They were Baby James, Frog, Tay Sicko, Baby Lord, and Big Keanan, and they had arrived in two black-out Escalades about an hour after the failed attempt on Markio's life. The trucks were the ESV models, stretched long and wide and capable of seating seven comfortably.

Those bulletproof Escalades had cost Marko $300, 000 apiece.

His iPhone chimed with a FaceTime alert. It was Black Reggie, his best friend in the whole 219 area code. He answered, and the video image that appeared on his phone screen was a camera panning across a thick blue carpet that was covered in assault rifles. AR-15s and AR pistols. AK-47s and Dracos. Below those were MAC-10s and MAC-11s with 50-shot clips, then Glock pistols with 50-shot drum magazines.

"Yeeeah, nigga," Markio said, nodding his head emphatically as Black Reggie switched the camera view to his bald black head. "You get the lo on buddy yet?"

The "lo" meant the location, and Black Reggie said, "Aw, you already know. The nigga stay right on top'a the Eighth Street hill. Same house Mike Cain and his people used to stay in. ain't no need to spin through there, though. He ain't up there. They say Nubby left the hospital and went straight to Chicago. Didn't even stay long enough to see no detectives."

"Did you just say Nubby?"

"That's the name he go by now."

"Ain't no way in hell I'd let a nigga call me nubby."

Black Reggie chuckled as he raised a plump brown blunt to his full black lips. He puffed and spoke with the thick gray smoke billowing out of his mouth.

"Lil hood bitch named Bambi picked up the shells y'all left behind. I looked out for her. Some pregnant White bitch who works at the Gucci store says she accidentally deleted all the data from the parkin' lot cameras. They arrested her for obstruction. I found out who her baby daddy was and gave him the bond money. Gave Nika that bread too. You owe, nigga."

Markio blinked and exhaled his relief. "I gotchoo, my nigga. On Vice Lord, I gotchoo." He couldn't repress the smile. "Back to this nigga Pudgy, though. Or Nubby. Whatever the fuck. I know he kicked it with somebody. Who he be wit'? How he find out I was at that mall?"

"We still tryin'a figure that out. Let me do some investigatin'. I'll hitchoo back."

Markio gave a nod and ended the video call. Then he was back online, taking swallows from his bottle of Fiji water while he perused the mainstream news sites.

"Why do you keep checking your phone?"

He looked up from his phone and beamed a smile that spanned the full width of his mouth. Morena was a little over halfway dry, and she'd tied a big white Versace towel around her waist, effectively covering her fat jiggly ass from all the sneaky eyes that kept staring at it.

Markio glanced around for Brittany and Amanda and found them at the bar, chatting it up with the bartender.

"Your phone," Morena repeated. "You keep checking it. Why?"

"Sit down." He patted the seat beside him. Chief Sosa, dozing at the opposite end of the sofa, opened his eyes and turned his head to see what all the thumping was about.

Morena sat down next to Markio. She looked at Chief Sosa, stroked the fur on his back while she talked to Markio.

"I really don't like having my questions ignored. You're looking at all the news sites. Which means you hit that boy you shot at and you're trying to see if he died and if you're wanted for shooting him." She swiveled her beautiful head on her slender neck and stared at Markio with her clear brown eyes. "Well, he died. I'll clear that up for you now. Can't say that I blame you for it either. Jesus, that was so *scary*. I've never been shot at in my *life*."

"It ain't that big of a deal."

"I call bullshit."

Markio laughed.

"Don't laugh. There's nothing funny about being shot at. It is a very big deal."

"Not when all of your cars are bulletproof, and you got five niggas in the two foreigns right behind you wit' glizzies and chop sticks. Security don't get no better than that."

"Your security didn't hop out until the shooter was already speeding off."

"Happened too fast." Markio shrugged his shoulders. On his phone he went from MSNBC to Fox News. from Fox to CNN.

"Even if the news media does get wind of that shooting, I highly doubt it'll be on the pages you're looking at."

"It will be if they find out an Oscar-nominated screenwriter was involved. Especially a Black one."

Morena had nothing to say to that. She scratched at Chief Sosa's back until he rose up and bounded onto her lap, where he rolled over on his side to expose his belly for a rub. Morena gave him that rub. It made his rear left leg work like a kid trying to speed up on a skateboard. Morena giggled.

Then she tied her wet, curly hair back and said, "You got all your family in here, and you wanna sit over here checking your phone. Don't be an old man."

"Old man?" Markio stood up and unpocketed a few items. A thirty-thousand-dollar stack of hundreds, the key to his Phantom, the keys to the beach house, his wallet. "You just called me an old man." He said it in wavering tones of disbelief as he placed the things he'd taken from his pockets on the glass-topped coffee table with his phone. "I'll show you an old man."

"Boy, you better go on somewhere," Morena said, laughing.

Markio scooped her up and folded her over his shoulder. He smacked her on the ass as she struggled laughingly against the strength of his arm. He kicked off his Louis Vuitton sneakers and took off running toward the swimming pool. Morena shrieked. Chief Sosa chased after them, barking like a mad dog. *Let's get her ass*, that bark said. The canine equivalent of what Smokey said to Craig just before they chased down Lil Chris.

Up in the air and down into the water they went, and that was the beginning of Markio's shift toward a genuinely good mood. He went down the water slide. He caught Brittany and Amanda lacking next to the pool and dunked them both at the same time, and then, not even ten minutes later, he did the same thing to his sisters, Mariah and Shakia. He played spades with family and shot dice with friends, and when the chef and his assistant were done preparing dinner everyone went to the dining room and sat at the twenty-seat cherry wood dining table. There were more asses than chairs, so the housekeeper, Mrs. Nettles, showed the yacht crew where more chairs were located.

The dinner was superb. Perfectly seasoned and seared quail with sweet watermelon molasses and delicious cornbread dressing. A colorful succotash with rice, four-cheese macaroni, oven roasted chicken, vegan burritos, steak taco, freshly squeezed lemonade. The works.

Markio ate with a smile on his face and a joy in his heart, all the while keeping his iPhone face down on the table, two or three inches away from his elbow. Every once in a while he picked it up to check the news. Nothing on the Lighthouse Mall shooting yet, but that wasn't what he was looking for anyway.

All evening long he'd been checking the news sites for any signs of Herb, because when Herb struck, it always made the world news.

Chapter 12

Watching Herbert Harris smile was a uniquely frightening thing to witness. Even to an audience of four Chicago policemen who had over the span of their respective careers seen men with their skulls blown open from high-caliber rifle rounds, entire families charred and smoking in their burned-out vehicles, tiny children flattened in the street like roadkill.

Herb's smile was a deeper horror. He smiled with his head tilted malevolently forward. Only his mouth and the wrinkles surrounding it moved. The rest of his face remained frozen in black ice.

"He's in our crosshairs," Herb said. He kept looking from the selfie photograph on the screen of the smartphone in his hand to the four men who were standing and sitting around the living room. "Tonight is the night, baby. No more Millionaire Markio. Tick tock, tick tock, tick tock …"

The selfie showed Kolita standing ear to ear with Markio Earl. She was wearing that ignorant diamond chain she'd taken from one of the girls at the Lincoln Park mansion. Markio had on three of them. He was holding up his fingers in a hand sign that looked kind of like a peace sign but was really a gang sign. Herb knew that the two raised fingers represented the ears of a rabbit, something about swiftness, but he was no expert on Vice Lord literature.

The room smelled like Officer Kolita Pierre. Herb shut his eyes and filled his lungs with her tantalizing fragrance…

until a raunchy fart from one of the cops contaminated the air.

Knee-slapping laughter ensued. Herb popped his eyes open and glowered. Officer Austin, the runt of the litter, was the culprit. He was a featherweight of a man, maybe a hundred and thirty pounds on his heaviest day, and he was shorter than the man they were after, maybe five two in his thick-soled boots – and that was a *strong* maybe, like a queen of hearts in a game of Spades.

The other three cops were Rice, Meredith, and Storms. Rice was bulky and bronze, almost Samoan in appearance. He had five children with his ex-wife and three more with his new old lady. A lot of bellies to fill, and school clothes to buy, and field trips to pay for. A million dollars, all tax-free and off the books, would hold him over for a good long while.

Meredith was the confused sort of man who would have been booted off the police force when Herb was coming up in the mid-1900's. Built like a bog of wet potatoes, he was a red-headed white man who wanted to be a red-headed white woman. No one understood why he wanted a sex change, since he claimed to only be attracted to women, and frankly Herb didn't care. All that mattered was that Officer Kyle Meredith needed the money to get some surgeon to turn his dick and balls into a pussy, and to stuff in a decent pair of tits to go with it. With a million dollars, the chubby faggot might be able to turn himself into Lucille Ball.

And then there was Larry Storms. Another faggot. He'd been a lieutenant with the Chicago Police Department until some questionable observer found him on OnlyFans with a fat black dick in his mouth. He was in uniform, so the Department came down hard on him. He'd lost his stripes. His wife had filed for divorce. Soon he would be fired from the force, and the brawny old freak would have to move far away to start a new life. A million dollars would put him in a great position to restart.

Kolita had picked them well.

"So what's next?" Storms asked. All gruff and serious. "We got the bastard in our sights. Pierre knows where he's at. What else do you want form us?"

"Yeah," Austin concurred. "We located the guy hours ago. You're literally looking at a picture one of our officers took with the guy. That was the deal, right?" He turned to the others. "Wasn't it? We track down Millionaire Markio, we get the money." Back to Herb. "So where's the dough? Four million for us, and two million more for Titus and Pierre."

"For real," Officer Rice said. "Show me the money."

"Telemundo," Meredith added, for some dumb reason.

Herb slipped the phone into the side pocket of his fitted Armani slacks and leaned forward on the blonde wood handle of his cane. His smile was unwavering. A fly buzzed down and landed on the bridge of his nose, and he left it there to tickle his skin as he scanned the room.

"You know," he said, after a time, "there's this old saying. Patience is a virtue. Ever heard it?"

"Sergeant Martin's gonna be all over our asses if we're not back in Chicago by sunrise." Austin kept flipping a quarter into the air with his thumbnail and catching it in his little hand. "I say you hand over the cash so we can split."

"As soon as I get Markio."

"That wasn't the deal," Officer Storms said. He stuck out his chest. The toughest cock-smoker in town.

Herb said, "Deal was, you lead me to Markio. That was the deal, and that hasn't happened. A groupie photo with him is not an address. I want *him*. I want *Markio*."

Hot white spittle chased behind that final word. *Markio*. In his mind that name was framed in fire, and the rage in his veins was the fuel that fed the conflagration. Soon those hellish flames would burn so hot that Millionaire Markio would simply sizzle out of existence.

"You got a fly on your nose," Meredith said.

And as if the fly had actually heard and understood that the sexually confused redhead had just snitched him out, it took off for higher ground and landed on the smooth brim of Herb's jet black Stetson.

Officer Austin raised his left hand like a student in class. He was still flipping his coin and catching it in his right hand. He was dressed like his pals, in tan combat boots and camouflage cargo pants and a brown tee shirt. Looking like the narcs they were.

"You ever seen *It*?" Meredith asked Herb. "that Stephen King movie, with the killer clown? Pennywise? You would've aced that role. You got that creepy smile down packed."

Herb ignored the compliment. He looked over to Austin without moving his head. "What do you want, meatball?"

"Just wondering why you asked us to meet you here to begin with if it wasn't to give us the dough. I mean, we were staked out all around town, watching some of Millionaire Markio's last known hangouts, and you pulled us out before we could get any solid leads. Not a wise move, you ask me. He might've pulled into Lakeland Projects two minutes after I drove off."

The left-right wag of Herb's head was barely perceptible. "He ain't in no projects. He took his woman shoppin' for a bathing suit. Means water. I had Titus go and hang out at the beach. No sign of him there, either. No boats out on the water. Nothin'. Few people said they've seen him walkin' a little black dog through the sand some mornings, but nobody's seen him out there today. So we're left to wait until he links up with his boy Loochie, which should be any time now. Kolita's there with Loochie now. They're all playing dominoes at a house not far from here. As soon as he gets there he's dead. Then you'll get your money. Then and only then."

Austin caught his quarter and stared at Herb for a long moment. Herb stared back. The fly got bored and flew off.

Five feet behind Herb, on the widescreen television, a country boy sang a country song about a country girl in a bar.

Finally Storms said, "What if something happens to you during this little mission of yours?"

"Kolita knows where the money is," Herb said.

Meredith looked around at his fellow officers. He was seated in an armchair with his legs femininely crossed and his lips poised like a faggot. He wore light brown lipstick that matched his gear and dark black mascara that matched his hellbound soul.

"You know," he said, practically singing the word *know*, "we could just keep Mr. Harris here and contact the FBI. They're offering *ten* million for his arrest."

"Yo, you fuckin' stupid?" Officer Rice gave Meredith a well-deserved slap to the back of the head.

"Law enforcement can't collect on bounties," Storms explained.

"Plus, you know," Austin added, "we aided this guy in a double murder last week. You forget about that?" He turned back to Herb just as Herb was turning towards the door. "Hey. wait a second. You still haven't answered my question."

"I'll call you in a couple of minutes."

Herb opened the door and stepped out into the hallway. The carpet was red with gold accents and the walls were bone white and the ceiling was gold. A faint aroma of sugary pastries hung in the air. Herb went to the elevator and used a knuckle to press the button with the downward facing arrow, supporting himself on a cane he didn't really need. When the chromium doors parted, he stopped in and turned around and stared down the hall until the doors closed in front of him.

"Pigs," he said, studying his reflection. "Can't live with 'em, but they make for good bacon."

He wore a dark blue Armani shirt with a silk tie that was gray like his Stetson hat. His Beretta pistol was stowed in a tan leather holster on his left hip. It was the same .45 he'd used to murder the Slauson brothers, but he had no plans to use it on Markio.

He knuckled the button for the lobby and then closed his eyes and reveled in the moment of sure and serene freedom as the cool metal box transported him through the lower floors. It had been months since he'd taken the risk of venturing outdoors without a disguise. Last Sunday was the first time he'd done it . and now today. Two Sundays in a row. Like weekly religious services.

"Let the church say Amen," he said, in his loudest voice.

"*Amen*," he answered for the imaginary congregation.

There was an electronic *ding*. Then the elevator doors spread open like doors to a robot heaven and out Herb walked.

The lobby had the same carpet as the upstairs hallways, a red and gold runway that began outside the elevators and ended at the second set of glass double doors forty-five feet away. Here the air smelled like perfume and popcorn. On his left Herb passed four vending machines filled with fun things for fat people. Two corpulent white girls stood at one machine, the pale one pointing out items while the tanned one dropped in quarters. Neither of them acknowledged the old Black man who walked past behind them.

Behind the receptionist's desk was a coffee-brown woman with lips and hips for days and days. She was leaning back in her swivel chair, examining the multicolored fingernails on her right hand and using her left hand to feed popcorn into her sexy mouth, all while talking into the office phone she had wedged between her shoulder and ear. She offered Herb a smile and a wave as he came into view, and he saw that her fingertips were all oily from the butter. He tipped his hat and continued on.

Off to the right and directly across from the receptionist's desk was a large waiting area with big windows looking out on the parking lot. The chairs had thick burgundy faux leather cushions and black tubular arms that arched down to become legs. A well-dressed family of Mexicans - four young women and an older gentleman – sat on one side of the U-shaped arrangement of chairs, looking at their phones and talking in rapid-fire Spanish. A young Black woman was seated on the opposite side of the room from the Mexican clan. She was maybe twenty-two, a beautiful girl with reddish brown skin and brick red lips, wearing a velvety orange bodysuit and strappy black high-heeled shoes that showed off her very pretty feet. Her necklace was like the one Kolita had on, only it was gold, and there were no white diamonds crushed and sprinkled all through it. She looked bored, slouched over to the side with her elbow on the arm of the chair and her fist pressed into her jaw. Whatever she was swiping through on her iPhone clearly was not amusing. Her hair was golden brown with a part up the middle, and a few long strands of it hung down over her left eye.

Herb stopped at the first set of double-doors. Her chair was three feet to the right of the doors. She looked over at Herb, to see why he had stopped to look at her. The hair fell from in front of her eye, and Herb saw that it was dead. A gray iris and a gray pupil. She sucked her teeth and sighed and said, "Can I help you?"

"Uh … Yeah." Herb had kept a big wad of folded cash in his pocket for the past four or five decades. He'd learned early on that cash money was the most convincing form of persuasion known to man. He dragged an impressive knot of hundred-dollar bills out of his right-hand pocket, transferred the cash to his left hand, and then dug in the same pocket and came out with the key to his Bentley. "I need a driver. Just for a couple of hours. I'll pay you a couple hundred."

The dead-eyed beauty hooked her arm through the loops of her black Michael Kors purse and walked to Herb in a n instant. Her pensive frown flipped over faster than Simone Biles off a balance beam.

"Sure, I'll drive you. Where you wanna go?"

"Just around. A few places. I'll point the way."

He gave her the Bentley key and two crisp hundreds, and she went out head of hill. Following her outside, he caught the scent of good perfume and apple shampoo. Her bodysuit was kind of loose-fitting, but it did nothing to hide her big wobbling butt. Herb grinned at the view.

The sun had laid down to rest, but it had left the heat behind. A sweltering blast of it fell over Herb like a heated blanket, and the dead-eyed beauty said, "Oh my Jesus. See, this is the kind of heat where a bitch just says no. as in, like, 'No, I don't wanna gang out. No, I don't wanna lay up with you. No, I don't wanna fuck or kiss or cuddle.' That's what this weather brings out of me."

Herb said nothing.

His Bentley was parked right up against the front of teh hotel, in a handicap-designated parking space, because he had a handicap sticker on his front windshield. The car was a 2024 Mulsanne with glossy black exterior paint, black rims, and black interior leather. Even the windows were nearly black. "Open up that back door for me," Herb said, and pointed his cane at the rear passenger's side door. He watched her butt rock and wobble like a pumpkin made of gelatin as she went to the door and pulled it open."

"You need some help getting in?"

"Nahhh. I done had two hip replacements. Went to those good Hollywood doctors. They fixed me up real good. I can still get a mile on the treadmill most mornings. I may be old, but I'm in shape."

He proved it by lifting the can off the ground as he walked to the open door and climbed in. Standing there outside his door, the pretty girl with one lively brown eye and one dead gray one smiled and nodded with her whole body and said, "Okay, I see you. I see you, old school. Okay. Show 'em what they ain't know." She giggled sweetly. A bead of sweat that had formed in the hollow of her throat snaked a path down to her chest and vanished between the ample swells of her breasts.

She pushed the door gently shut and hurried around to the driver door. Herb could almost feel his flesh cooking against the hot leather seat. As soon as the dead-eyed beauty got in behind the wheel, he urged her to start the engine and get the air-conditioning going. She was equally hungry for cool air, so she wasted no time in following his instruction.

"Ooouuu, yes Lord. *Wooo!* Sweet relief." She chuckled weakly and looked back at him. "I'm Vielle, by the way. Vielle Gaing. That's Gaing as in G-A-I-N-G. Lotta people misspell it."

"And you're from?"

"Oh, I'm from Houston, Texas. Fifth Ward. My auntie raised me down there 'cause my daddy been in jail since I was two, and my mama a junkie. I moved out here in April to get a job and a house for my daddy to come home to, 'cause he'll be comin' home later this year, and he can't live with my brother. Pops gon' be on parcel, you know for two whole years. And my brother's a cop." She shook her head at something and shifted the transmission into Reverse. "I was waiting on bro to come and pick me up, but he got tied up in some kind of homicide investigation. Some dude got killed over there by the Lighthouse Mall a few hours ago. I mean, he got shot over there, but he died at the hospital. Saint Anthony's. They think Millionaire Markio or one of his boys might've done it because –"

"Markio?" Herb's cordial expression hardened, but Vielle failed to notice it. She was turned in her seat, her one good eye focused on the rear window as she backed the blacked-out Bentley sedan out of the blue-lines handicap parking slot.

"Mm hm. They call him Millionaire Markio. He's the guy that old man was after when…" Veille trailed off. She pressed her high-heeled shoe down on the brake pedal and brought the Mulsanne to a slow, almost thoughtful halt. Recognition wrinkled her brow.

"Something wrong? You look like you seen a ghost." Herb had taken two smartphones out of his left-hand pocket and laid them end to end on the armrest next to him, but he wasn't looking at them. He was looking at Vielle. Looking her in the eye, so to speak.

"You're that man," she said. "The one the FBI's been looking for. You killed those boys in Chicago last week."

"I am, and I did. Speaking of which, what were you doing waiting in that hotel lobby? You staying here?"

"No."

"No? Then who were you waiting on? And don't say your brother."

"A friend of mine." She swallowed some spit and waited eight seconds before adding, "I think he stood me up."

Herb nodded twice and picked up both smartphones. "One second," he said, and dialed Officer Austin's number on one phone while manually typing a second ten-digit area code and phone number on the other phone. Austin answered on the first ring.

"Let me guess, Pennywise. You want us to run interference so you can nail this asshole and get away with it. That's why you had us meet you here at the hotel, wasn't it?"

"Not even close."

Herb ended the call with Austin and hit the green *call* button on the second phone.

The explosion was deafening.

Eight pounds of C4-explosion, wired to a prepaid smartphone and stuck to the back of the widescreen television, detonated all at once. The blast incinerated the four crooked policemen, wiped out two whole floors, and sent a glorious plume of fire rolling out of a huge smoking crater in the side of the building.

Shattered brick and glass began to rain down onto the Bentley. Vielle slumped low in her seat and made a sound in her throat that was not unlike a highly aroused moan.

"Drive," Herb said.

Vielle slammed the transmission into Drive, spun the steering wheel, and drove.

Chapter 13

"I'ma need fifty more o'dem blocks," Slime said.

He had just appeared in the doorway to Markio's bedroom. He was carrying a large gray leather duffel, the muscles in his lean right arm struggling with its bulk. Slime walked in and dropped the bag on the floor in front of Markio's left foot. It thumped down on the thick gray carpet and settled like the carcass of a small fat seal.

The "blocks" he was referring to were kilograms of uncut heroin that Markio purchased from the Matamoros drug cartel for $20,000-a-ki and resold wholesale for $70,000-a-ki. At least that was his usual wholesale price. For Slime; his cousin, Markio, had lowered the price of a kilo to $50,000.

Markio had just showered to get all the chlorinated water off his body. He'd changed into a pair of Louis Vuitton boxers, new black Balenciaga sweatpants, and plain white socks. No shirt. No chains. No twinkling rings or watches. All his jewelry lay on the cherrywood nightstand to his right, lit up by the shaded Italian lamp. The ache in the back of his left shoulder had returned. He was grimacing and rotating his left arm with his elbow folded in and his hand suspended loosely in front of the Chicago bulls tattoo he had inked into the skin of his left pectoral muscle.

"That's two and a half million?" Markio asked.

"You already know, five. Two and a half on the nose. I was gon' bring you one and a quarter and ask for the other twenty-five on consignment, but ain't no need to go dat route, ya heard me. Ain't no sense in makin' two money trips when I can just do it all at once."

Slime bent down to unzip the duffel and spread it open to show Markio the rubber-banded stacks of cash piled messily within it. Markio looked down into the bag and nodded. There was a lot of cash in there. All hundreds, by the looks of it. Two million and five hundred thousand dollars in Benjamins.

"Just dump it out on the carpet," Markio said. He lost his genuine grimace and forced a generic grin, clenching his teeth against the throbbing pain. "I'll have that fifty down in Baton Rouge by Wednesday. Unless you wanna drive it back yourself. In that case you can go and pick it up tonight. You'll have to drive out to Maywood, Illinois."

Slime took a moment to think. He sipped from the Styrofoam cup he was holding in his left hand and sucked his teeth. He stuck his right hand in his pants pocket and came out with a small rectangular container of Tic-Tacs. Only upon closer examination Markio saw that the container was half-filled with thirty-milligram tablets of Percocet. Slime thumbed open the lid and held it out toward Markio.

"Here, five. Pop you one'a these. Knock that pain right out."

"I'm good." Markio shook his head and winced at the stabbing ache the movement caused. "I'm good, bruh."

"Take one. You ain't gon' get high off no one pill."

"Gotta stay on my square, bruh. You saw what happened earlier. Niggas popped outta nowhere and tried to fan me down sit' a switch, faster than y'all could even react. Then I got this old man on my trail, and he can shoot from hundreds of yards away. Not to mention the feds. One slip up and I could lose my whole empire. Maybe even my life."

Slime inhaled and exhaled, nasally and dramatically, and said, "Okay. A'ight. But I want you to answer this one question. How you gon' shoot if your shoulder's all fucked up?"

He waited for an answer that Markio didn't have. After a couple of seconds Markio's generic grin became a genuine one. Then it widened into a defeated smile as he extended his hand, palm up, and accepted the two little tablets that Slime tapped out of the container. He used Slime's iced narcotic beverage to swallow one pill and pocketed the other one. The drink was promethazine with codeine and some kind of fizzing soda that made the whole concoction a snot green color. Markio had been addicted to Lean for almost two years. Opioids too. He'd put his body through hell quitting everything cold-turkey. That small sip he took from Slime's cup made him thirsty for more.

"We'll drive 'em back," Slime said, after a time. He tipped the duffel over and dumped its contents onto the soft gray carpet. "I got a snow bunny say she'll take that risk for a twenty, ya heard me. She from the north side of the Chi. Met her at a YB concert."

YB was code for NBA Youngboy. He and Slime and the other two Bloods Slime had brought with him were all from the same north side Baton Rouge neighborhood. They were often found in the background in the rap star's music videos, flashing guns and gang signs, smoking and sipping and mugging the cameras as if the nerdy white cameramen were the grimey black Crips who'd murdered their homies.

"I'll have the bros meet you out there in Maywood with that fifty," Markio said, reaching for his iPhone, which lay on the nightstand with his jewelry. "Be careful, nigga. Feds on our ass. Don't be out there takin' no unnecessary risks."

"Ball till you fall, you heard me."

"Fin Ball till you fall."

The two cousins smiled in unison. All the VVS diamonds on Slime's teeth glistened through more colors than there were in a rainbow. His cunning browneyes followed Markio's hand to the bedside table and lingered there, studying his cousin's jewelry.

"That Haitian vibe was icy as shit, wasn't she?" Slime said.

Markio's smile became a straight-lipped mask of contemplation. He looked up from his phone and gave a slow, deliberate nod. "That was strange, wasn't it? I mean, people who got enough money to afford jewelry like that usually move to bigger cities and stay there if they ain't already from there. Ice like that, she gotta be poppin' on the Gram. the fuck she doin' out here wit' my nigga Loochie?"

"Yeah … I was thinkin' that, too. She iced up like them reality TB bitches. Or like a female rapper. Somebody famous."

And that made Markio think of Cherish Taylor and Sasha the Stallion, the two reality TV stars from MTN's *The Real Baddies of Chicago* who'd been robbed of their jewelry just minutes before the Slauson brothers were shot and killed at that Lincoln Park mansion last Sunday.

"Maaaan," he said, and dialed FBS Longshot's phone number.

Slime said, "What?"

Markio shook his head and held up an index finger. The pain reliever was already working on his shoulder. He felt it a little, but the ache was distant now. Way out in New York City somewhere.

Jacobi Long answered halfway through the second ring. It was a FaceTime video call, and the first thing Markio noticed was that Jacobi's girlfriend had once again used his beard-trimmers to cut his unibrow into two separate eyebrows. Markio chalked that up to what the psychologists called "survivor's guilt". Jacobi had watched his two best friends get their brains blown out, and he'd only taken a bullet to the hip. Today he'd watched those same friends get lowered into the ground, and he'd returned home shortly thereafter with his heart still pumping blood and his brain still in working order.

"You should'a came to the funeral, bruh." Jacobi wet his lips and wiped fresh-tears from his eyes. "I know they mama didn't want you there, but you should'a came anyway. Lord n'em would'a wanted you to be there."

"I need to ask you some'n."

Jacobi dropped his head back and rubbed a hand down his face. When his head came forward again there were fresh tears in his eyes. Instead of wiping them away he blinked and let them roll down his cheeks.

"It's about that man, ain't it? It's about Herb."

"Kinda sorta."

"I gave him yo' old phone number. On bro. I did slip up and tell him what city you were in. Cherish did, too. She had heard it from Prinny. But we ain't give him no address. Couldn't even if we wanted to. Don't nobody know it."

Jacobi sniffed once and wiped his eyes twice, first with the heels of his hands and then with his index finger knuckles. *Hm,* Markio thought. *So that's what it was. Wasn't survivor's guilt after all. This nigga told Herb where to find me.*

Which meant that Herb and his crew were here in Michigan City, likely closing in on their target.

Jacobi was in bed; there was a gold upholstered headboard beyond his shoulders and a big pile of fluffy-black pillows behind his back. Audio form *The Real Baddies of Chicago* was playing in the background, which made more than enough sense. His girlfriend's sister, Cherish Taylor, was the biggest star of the show.

"I need you to think back to that night," Markio said, looking at Jacobi but reaching out for Slime's cup. Sometimes old habits die hard. The ache in his shoulder had crossed The Big Apple and was now riding the clouds somewhere over the Atlantic. "Think about the people Herb had with him."

Jacobi nodded his head like the dashboard toy in Ice Cube's *Are We There Yet?*" They had masks on, so ain't much I can really tell you."

"I just need to know if there was a woman. Try to remem—"

"Oh, yup. Yup. definitely was a woman. Short lil thick lil dark-skinned bitch. She the one took all the money and jewelry from everybody. My girl heard her voice in the house. She had some kinda accent."

Markio's smile could have turned water to ice.

He thanked FBS Longshot for the info and took another sip from the Styrofoam as he got up and went to his walk-in closet. Slime trailed him there, and a smart sensor turned on the lights when they entered the room. It was an impressively large closet, maybe eight hundred square feet of rich gray carpet with cherrywood shelves along the rear and right walls, parallel racks of high-end designer clothes off to the left, and thick glass display cases of expensive jewelry in the middle of the floor. The front walls were great big mirrors. The shelves on the back wall were slanted forty-five degrees downward, and there was a two-inch wooden barrier to keep Markio's extensive shoe collection from sliding off to the floor. The shelves on the right wall were level surfaces where all of Markio's tee shirts, boxer-briefs, and socks lay folded in neat, clean piles. He went there first, reaching back to return Slime's cup and seeing that Slime was brimming with excitement, so much so that he was bouncing on the toes of his green-and-white Gucci sneakers. The weed he'd smoked downstairs had his eyes red and squinted so narrowly that he could have been mistaken for a tall brown Chinese man. A diamond teeth samurai.

"*Slatt, slatt, slatt!*" said Slime, still bouncing as he took hold of his cup.

Nodding his head, not smiling at all, Markio pushed his head in through the collar of a new black Balenciaga tee and slipped his arms into the sleeves as he crossed the floor to grab a black pair of Nike Air Max '95 sneakers from the back wall.

"I *knew* it was some'n funny about that Haitian bitch," Markio said. The aggressive timbre of his voice revealed the rage within him. "I *felt* it. On TVL, I felt that shit in my veins. Shorty was way too friendly towards me, way too interested in meetin' me and hangin' out wit' me."

You already know what I say, five. It's northside, thirty-eighth. We put guns to the face. Who gon' die today."

That was another one of Slime's frequently voiced questions that was really more of a statement. It was a question/statement that Mariko had heard Slime's rap star homeboy, NBA Youngboy, repeat at the start and end of numerous chart-topping records.

Markio was still holding his iPhone. He put on a thin black hooded jacket to conceal the tattoos on his forearms, and he was just about to call Loochie when he got a text from Kisha, an ex-girlfriend of his from long ago. It read, *Please tell me you're not at the Marriott.* He replied, *Nah, I'm in bed at the crib.* Half fiction, half nonfiction. Then he got a FaceTime call from Black Reggie, and Chief Sosa came padding into the closet with his head held high and a bundle of hundred-dollar bills clenched between his teeth, and Morena appeared in the closet doorway, her pretty brown eyes all droopy and red-veined and focused on Markio's face.

"Amanda and Brittany were just called in to work," she said, as Markio pressed the button to accept the FaceTime from Black Reggie. "Someone just set off a bomb at some hotel. It's bad."

Markio responded to the news by grinding his teeth and breathing out through his nose, and though he found it difficult to peel his gaze off Morena - she too had showered, in the sprawling guest house that took up most of the west lawn, and she'd put those same skintight low-rise jeans back on, only instead of the purple tee she wore a red Gucci tee with matching running shoes – he forced himself to look away from her lust-inducing figure and down at the screen of his iPhone.

"Bruh, on Larry Hoover," Black Reggie said, because he was a Gangster Disciple, "these Fort Wayne niggas out her like twenty deep, and Nubby just pulled up wit' some niggas from yo' city. They know you used to trap out here on the west side, so that's where they posted up."

Where they at?"

"Remember the house Dawn and Strick used to live in? Right across from Park School?"

Markio nodded.

"That's where they're at. I just rode past 'em a minute ago."

Again Markio nodded. He could see that Reggie was driving. Every couple of seconds a streetlight would flash into the car and highlight the interior of the triple-black Challenger. The Hellcat motor roared and growled like Mufasa's evil feline brother.

"Meet me at the spot," Reggie said.

"On my way," Markio replied.

He ended the call and looked down at Chief Sosa. The little black dog had dropped the bundle of hundreds at his owner's feet and was now sitting down and looking up with his mouth open and his tongue put in a presumptuous little doggie smile that seemed to say *See what I found? Got a bone? We can trade!*

Markio squatted to pick up the cash and gave Chief a quick scratch behind the ears.

Woof! Woof! Woof! Chief barked. Which was doganese for *Where the fuck is my bone?*

Morena crossed her arms over her chest and leaned her shoulder against the jamb. "You've got way too much going on," she said. "And where'd you get all that money?"

"Book sales." Markio tossed her the bundle of Benjamins. "I'ma need you to house-sit for a couple hours. Maybe not even that long. Gotta tie up some loose ends."

"Loose ends. Hm." Her eyelids went even closer together, almost touching, and she drew her vapid pink lips to the side, stepping back into the bedroom as Markio and Slime breezed past her.

"I'll be back," Markio said.

"I hear you, terminator," Morena replied.

Markio chuckled thrice and kept on walking.

Chapter 14

Of the seventeen people gathered on the steeply sloping driveway next to Precious Tucker's somewhat dilapidated 7th Street home, only four of them were girls. Three of those girls were Tonya Byrd, Kela Sanders, and Bambi Middlebrooks, a trio of seventeen-year-olds who'd been best friends from Krueger Middle School all the way through to their freshman year at Michigan City High School, which was where their journey through the public school system came to an abrupt end that segued into their formal introduction to the criminal justice system.

And it was all Kela's fault

It was *always* Kela's fault.

The driveway was two long concrete tracks with a ragged line of weeds running between them. Most of the crowd was up near the garage, lingering around the tan-colored Jeep Wrangler 4X4 that Precious had gotten cheap from her one-handed older brother Nubby. Three of the Fort Wayne boys had followed the trio of besties down to the bottom of the driveway. One of them was a strong bull of a man with dreads for hair and diamonds for teeth. He was fanning out a big handful of cash, twenties and fifties mostly, and asking the girls how much it would cost to get them to join him and his boys in Precious's infamous basement, when Black Reggie's black-out Challenger went rumbling past a few minutes ago.

That was when Kela had opened her big fat mouth.

"Shit, y'all! There go one of Markio's guys right there! He the one who gave Bambi five hundred dollars just for pickin' up all the shells. I bet *he* can tell you where to find Markio."

Bambi's mouth fell open. So did Tonya's. They looked at each other with big-eyed incredulity. Then they looked at Kela, who was looking at the Fort Wayne boys, who had turned around to look at the passing muscle car.

"You dumbass bitch," Bambi said, just loud enough for Kela to hear.

The Challenger slowed to a stop at the Stop sign where 7th Street ended in a T-junction with Lincoln Avenue. At the same moment, Nubby's dark green Silverado pickup turned the corner from Lincoln onto 7th and braked right next to the Challenger.

Nubby's raving shouts were loud and resonant in the stillness of night. *"Tell dat bitch nigga I'm on his ass! Tell him I'm right here at my sista house!* And I got some'a *his* homeboys wit' me! I got fifty bands on his head! Fifty *bands!"*

Black Reggie had screeched off before Nubby was done shouting. All the commotion got the Fort Wayne boys excited. They came stampeding down the driveway, drawing guns with absurdly long clips, jumping into cars and trucks. Even Precious came shuffling down, big and brown and about as pretty as a werewolf in a summer dress.

"You need to quit drinkin', Kela." Tonya said, and smacked the red Solo cup out of Ke;a's hand. The cognac that was in it splashed across the sidewalk, a few droplets landing on Precious's ashy right foot and the buckled straps of her dirty white sandals.

Kela spun around to face her friends with her eyes wide and her hand cupped over her mouth. Like them, she was dressed for all the mess in a halter-top that ended well above her pierced navel, tight blue booty shorts that ended well above the lower swells of her fat black butt, and black low-top Air Force 1's. Her natural hair was tied up in two big Lady of Rage afropuffs. She had the darkest complexion of the three. She was also the heaviest, though neither of them were what anyone would call overweight.

Now Precious on the other hand - Precious was overweight. Her Aztec-patterned muumuu could have been mistaken for someone's lost window curtain. Her badly damaged hair was like a rough brown tumbleweed behind her knockoff Chanel headscarf, and she was patting away at an itch on the right side of her head as she watched Nubby's pickup pull to the curb behind Bambi's pastel blue Honda sedan.

Precious cut a glance at the girls and said, "What I tell y'all 'bout drinkin' and smokin' outside my house? Y'all tryna get me locked up?"

And as if on cue, two MCPD patrol cars veered around the corner from Lincoln Avenue and shot down 7th Street so fast that, a few seconds later, it was hard to remember them passing by at all.

Yet and still, the fleeting police presence had a sobering effect on the Fort Wayne boys. Some of them dropped their pistols and kicked them under the nearest vehicles. Engines that had just been fired up were switched off very suddenly. Nubby and three other men got out of the Silverado and stared up the street, in the direction the cop cars had gone, and when Bambi turned to look in that same direction she saw three more MCPD vehicles streak past on Willard Avenue.

"Damn, y'all, I swear to god, I did not mean to say that," Kela said, walking to the car. She leaned back against the rear passenger's side door, which was the door she'd gotten out of half an hour earlier.

Tonya, the silver-haired redbone, expressed her opinion with a blase roll of her silverish-gray eyes and a wag of her head. The wet suck of her teeth came two seconds later, but in the end all she said was, "did you see all that money he just flashed? That was alotta money. We might could'a got a band a piece to go down there and fuck them niggas. Prob'ly more than that."

"That's our rent money right there," Kela said.

"Rent, utilities, a new screen door." Tonya counted them off on her fingers. "And we'll still have enough left over to go and see Sexyy Red."

Bambi didn't comment. She was watching the bull of a man with dreads for hair and diamonds for teeth as he approached Nubby six feet up the sidewalk and said something she couldn't quite make out. The bull had introduced himself as T-Baby. He'd pulled up in the burnt orange Range Rover that was now parked halfway up Precious steep mountain of a driveway. The Rover had gold rims that were like thirty-inch-wide dinner plates.

Impressive, but not nearly as impressive as the two white Rolls-Royces she'd seen earlier in the day.

Nubby's pear-shaped head swiveled on his thick brown neck, and his irate eyes landed on Bambi. "Yeah? He tight with Markio, huh? Paid you for pickin' up the shells. A'ight." He nodded his pear, turned to his people, and said, "Y'all go and try to catch up with that Charger. Put a hun'ed holes in that motherfucka."

"That was a Challenger," someone corrected.

"Charger! Challenger! I don't give a fuck what it was! I got ten thousand for whoever kill the nigga that's drivin' it!"

Seconds later four cars started up and sped off down 7th Street, two vanishing down Lincoln Avenue and the other two racing toward Willard.

Bambi and Tonya finished off their Hennessy, and Tonya collected all three cups and dropped them into a neighbor's curbside trash bin, while Nubby, shaking with rage, walked up on Bambi and sneered in her pretty face.

"You fuck with them niggas?" His sweaty upper lip trembled with the accusation. "You cool with them niggas or some'n?" His thumb was wrapped in thick white gauze. His index and middle fingers were hooked under the loops of a white plastic Subway bag that Bambi could see was filled with stacks of hundred-dollar bills, the kind that came with gold paper wrappers.

"I know Black Reggie," Bambi said. "We buy our weed from him sometimes, and I know he's friends with Millionaire Markio. When I saw what went down at the mall, I picked up the shells so y'all could keep that shit in the streets. You should be thanking me."

"Period," Tonya said as she returned to Bambi's side.

Nubby meditated. Bambi waited.

"I'll tell you what," Nubby said, after seven silent seconds. "I got ten bands for you, right here in this bag, if you can tell me where we can find that nigga."

This time it was Bambi who meditated, and Nubby who waited. Precious and the three lanky Chicagoans who'd emerged from the Silverado with Nub moved to stand behind him. One of the men was so tall that Bambi could see right up into the double barrels of his nose. There was a portly gray booger clinging to the inner wall of his left nostril. Bambi saw it and grimaced and lowered her gaze back to Nubby's rabid sneer. Kela pushed off the car but kept the soles of her Nikes planted firmly on the curb, not watching Tonya or Bambi but watching the three rangy black men and Nubby and the muumuu-wrapped refrigerator he called a sister.

"We ain't never been to Markio's house," Bambi said finally. "I know he's in town, though. He's somewhere out here. If anybody *can* find him, though, it would be us. We're from here, born and raised. We know everybody."

"She ain't lying, big bro," said the sister who was three times bigger than the big bro. She was still patting the side of her head. "Bambi knows everybody 'round here."

"Give us a thousand dollars apiece," Bambi said, "and we'll be out here lookin' for his ass all night.

She thought there would be another tense moment of contemplation from Nubby, but he handed the Subway bag to Precious as soon as the offer was made and told her to count out the three grand.

While Precious counted, Bambi flicked her eyes up and down the dark street, which was lit well enough by the towering street lights but was still gloomy and shadowy. Another cop car went streaking past on Willard, this one with its jackpot lights flashing and its siren blipping. Bambi furrowed her brow, wondered where all those cops were on their way to, and then continued her visual sweep of the street.

The time of night was nearing eleven, and there were still a few houses with jaundiced yellow light glowing in the windows. A crackhead called Pipemaster pedaled by on a ten speed and shouted to a slender brown woman who was standing on a porch three houses down, smoking a cigarette, but Bambi didn't catch what he shouted. Something about a hotel. Whatever it was made the woman raise her smartphone and turn on the screen, illuminating her face as she went swiping for information.

Across the street there was a low brick building that had once been called Park Elementary School but was now the Tristan Walker Youth Center. No lights in those big rectangular windows. No rubbery bounces or masculine shouts from the fenced-in basketball courts out back. The center closed at three on Sundays.

Precious handed over the cash and asked Nubby where he'd gotten all that money while Bambi went to her Honda and got in behind the wheel. Tonya got in next to her, and Kela got in behind Tonya. Bambi was turning the key behind her steering wheel and staring at a long black Escalade that had just turned off of Willard and onto 7th Street when Nubby walked over to her window and tapped a knuckle on the glass. An ashy knuckle. Not the sort of knuckle you'd expect to see on a man with eighty or ninety grand in a Subway bag.

Bambi lowered her window. "Let me give you some free game," she said, before he could even speak. "Markio is, like … he's one of those real street niggas, one of those real Chicago gang members who'll kill you in a heartbeat. Remember when G-Money got killed right back there off 7th and Willard a few years ago? Markio did that. They can't prove it, but my girl Vielle's brother is a cop, and he said they *know* Markio did it. In fact, he said they're investigating Markio for a *number* of murders, seven or eight of 'em, and he said every person Markio gets into it with ends up dead soon after."

"You think I give a fuck about how many bodies that nigga got?"

"I didn't say you did. All I'm sayin' is, Markio ain't for none, and you just sent all your boys, all your *shooters*, to try and catch that fast ass car Black Reggie got, which leaves you kinda vulnerable, don't you think?"

In a matter of milliseconds, Nubby's hard, scrunch-faced mask of vengeance softened and spread out into a wary look of stunned trepidation. He took a step back and glanced left, at the two harmless teenage boys who'd just rounded the corner from Lincoln Avenue.

He was looking the wrong way.

Had he glanced to his right, he'd have seen what Bambi spied in her rearview mirror as she made a hasty U-turn in the street.

A second black Escalade had just turned off of Willard Avenue and onto 7th Street, and now both SUVs were speeding down the street with their headlights off.

Bambi sped off from the curb, hunched forward over the steering wheel. Her friends, who'd also started watching the street behind them - Tonya in her side-mirror, Kela looking back over her seat - reached in similar fashion, slouching low, making themselves small as their sedan went rocketing toward Lincoln Avenue.

"*Goooo, go!*" Kela said, unconsciously imitating their favorite rapper Lil Durk's go-to adlib.

They were making a hard left turn onto Lincoln when the harsh rattle of fully automatic gunfire began.

Chapter 15

"That's him! That's him right there! Bail out!"

Markio gave the order as he shoved open the rear driver's side door of the lead SUV and bailed out himself, holding a Glock pistol with a 50-round drum magazine and a switch that enabled the gun to fire like a machinegun. Buck, Kay, slime, Bloody Money, and Bee Baby hopped out of the same sport utility vehicle, with Buck and Kay aiming their Draco pistols and the Bloods brandishing the modified Glocks Slime had picked up from a side chick's apartment in Chicago shortly after his flight had landed.

The Fin Ball Shortiez – Big Keanan, Tay Sicko, baby James, Baby Lord, and Frog, all Traveling Vice Lords from Chicago North Lawndale neighborhood – were in the second Escalade. Big Keanan, whose gun Markio had borrowed, stayed in the driver's seat, but the other four leapt out wearing gloves and ski-masks and wielding fully automatic firearms.

Ten men with five Glocks and five Century Arms Draco pistols. Over four hundred rounds of ammunition.

They turned West 7th Street into a tight show.

The only survivor was a fat ugly woman wearing a loose, brightly colored dress, and she even suffered numerous bullet wounds in the hailstorm of gunfire.

While the others chased after and gunned down Nubby's three amigos, Markio, Slime, and Baby Lord ran at Nubby, shooting him to the ground as they went, and when they got to him they stood over him and emptied their guns into his face, turning his bald brown pear into a smashed red tomato.

The two Cadillac Escalades raced off twenty-two seconds after they pulled up.

Chapter 16

"So tell me the truth," Herb rasped, after he'd taken a deep drag from his Pall Mall cigarette and exhaled. "Who were you waiting for in that hotel lobby? Your drug-dealer? Your pimp? I know it wasn't a cop."

Wasn't waiting on you, Vielle thought. *That's for damn sure.*

The thought came to her encrusted with a complex filigree of emotion: uneasiness, horror, the all-encompassing fear of what was to come. A cold bead of sweat that felt something like liquid ice went trickling down the middle of her back. Her breath came in shaky hitches, as if each inhalation were really a series of much smaller ones, ten or fifteen of them stacked one on top of the other.

She chewed in her bottom lip and stared down at the Facebook news feed on the screen of her smartphone. It was her only method of escape. The old man was seated behind the passenger's seat, with a clear view of her, and he watched her every move.

They were parked on a short side street next to Southgate Apartments. Both sides of the street were lined with nice single-story homes. Neatly manicured lawns, picket fences made of pine and oak and bland ash separating the property lines, upright trash bins and unlittered driveways and fun recreational things like trampolines and above-ground swimming pools decorating the front yards. Aside from the low vibration of music emanating from a white clapboard house toward the far end of the street and the occasional shriek of sirens as police cars and fire trucks and boxy red-on-white ambulances zipped past on the perpendicular street behind them, the only sounds to be heard were the mating calls of crickets and frogs in the rich green grasses that beautified this dreamy expanse of single-family homes.

"Come on," Herb urged. "Give it to me, who were you waiting on?"

Vielle hesitated, then, with a shrug and a suck of her teeth, she said, "My brother really is a cop, but you're right, I wasn't waiting on him. I was supposed to be meeting up with this guy. Charlie Byrd. When I first moved her from Texas, I met these three girls at that BP gas station on Michigan Boulevard. Tonya, Bambi, and Kela. We been cool ever since, even though they're all four years younger than I am. Anyway, when my car got repossessed, Tony's daddy started taking me to work some mornings, and sometimes he'd pick me up after my shift and take me out to eat before he dropped me off."

"Smart man."

"*Gullible* man. He fell right into my trap. I could've easily gotten a ride from one of my coworkers – especially from Jack, Jack Davis, he'd drive me to Mexico if he thought he'd get some pussy out of it – but I let Charlie do it, 'cause he owns two duplexes and another rental property that bring inn almost five grand very month. Plus he's a carpenter, makes like twenty-eight dollars an hour. I charge him three *hundred* an hour, we've been doing that like four or five times a month, and he was supposed to meet me at the Marriott tonight but he stood me up."

"So you're a whore."

Vielle snapped a cold glance at Herb. His head and neck were so dark that they seemed to blend with the black leather of his seat. The whites of his eyes and teeth stood out in bright, exclamatory clarity. He puffed on his cigarette and inhaled.

"Don't come for me, old man. Okay? Because I'll give you this money back and call me an Uber."

Herb exhaled out his open window, streaming the smoke out the side of his mouth. "Didn't mean no harm by it. Just an observation, that's all. Nothin' wrong with prostitution Government needs to go on and legalize it, you ask me."

"Everybody sells pussy where I come from," Vielle said, turning back to her phone. "My mama and all five of her sisters, they're all from Fifth Ward too, the northeast side of Houston, and every one of them done sold some pussy before. Some of 'em still do. So naturally it passed down to their daughters. I started seven years ago. When I was fourteen. Had a baby Benz by the time I was sixteen, my own apartment, all the designer shit you can name. Me and two of my Auntie Labri's daughters, my cousins Shelly and Rayna, worked the Motel 6 on Katy Freeway. I was clearing fifteen hundred a night, sometimes more than that. I got my daddy a lawyer, sent his mama and his sister money when they needed it. Every two weeks I would fly out to Chicago and link up with my daddy's side of the family, then I'd get with my sister Flower and my brother Lord and we'd drive out here to Indiana State Prison for that lil two-hour visit. Every couple of visits. I'd smuggle in some drugs – two or three ounces of coke here, and an ounce or two of H there, you know. We never got caught or anything. He didn't like me doing it, but I did it anyway, and he'd always pay me back and use the profit to take care of his kids."

"Your father's from Chicago?"

"Mm hm," Vielle nodded, glancing up and into the rearview mirror as two mor MCPD vehicles went lancing by on Ohio Street. A motley mob of four women and three men were gathered at the corner back there, watching the first responders streak past and wondering what caused the enormous explosion that had clearly stunned most of them out of bed. "My, uhh, my daddy's whole family, they're all from Chicago. The west side mostly, but they're all over the city, from Austin and Lawndale to Englewood and Roseland."

"What's his name?"

This time when Vielle looked at the rearview mirror her eye was on the elderly lone wolf terrorist sitting behind her. He was holding a pair of Nikon night vision binoculars up to his eyes, watching the far end of the street ahead, presumably the house where there was music playing.

"Hardis," Vielle said, after a time. "His name is Hardis."

Herb lowered his binoculars and swung his head to look at Vielle so suddenly that his Stetson went askew and a bone in his neck crackled like a handful of wet Rice Krispies. He fixed his hat and rubbed the side of his neck and stared at Vielle with his eyebrows raised high, creating a densely compacted family of wrinkles across his panther black forehead.

"What?" Vielle's quizzical squint only wrinkled the skin in between her eyebrows. "Why you lookin' at me like that? You know my daddy or some'n?"

"Hardis ..." Herb's raspy voice took on a wondrous, disbelieving tone. His eyes ticked left and right, down and up, studying her face as if he knew her, as if he'd seen her before. Then he showed his teeth in an oddly straight-lipped grin, shook his head, and let loose a cackling laugh that made all the hairs on the nape of Vielle's neck stand out like the quills on a porcupine's back.

Keck-keck-keck-keck-keck.

A hellish laugh if ever there was one.

"You're a creepy old nigga, you know that?"

He answered her question with one of his own. "Hardis Black, right? From Rockwell Gardens?"

"Black is his middle name. His last name is Gaing, like mine."

"And he's been in prison this whole time?"

Vielle nodded. "Ever since oh-five. Dirty-ass cop named Maxie framed him for a murder he didn't even do."

'No jive?" Another incredulous shake of his black leather head. "No wonder I ain't been able to track him down all these years. I was lookin' for Hardis Black." he wrestled the huge fold of bills back out of his pocket, started to thumb through it, then changed his mind and reached out to Vielle with the whole big pile clutched loosely in his charcoal hand. "Here you go. Take out whatever you need and send the rest to your old man. Tell him ol' herb said we'll have a drink at Papi't Place whenever them white folks free him."

"Papi's Place?"

"Yeah. Papi's Place. He'll know what I mean." All at once, Herb smiled, nodded, raised his binoculars, and cursed Vielle's ears with another burst of cackling chitters.

It sounded more like an alien language than any laugh she'd ever heard, and when this nightmare night was over, that strange, cold, dark, malevolent cackle would haunt her dreams for years to come.

Vielle spent the next couple of minutes counting and recounting the fat pile of hundreds, which amounted to $14, 600, which washed away her fears and made her smile like a beautiful fool.

Maybe five minutes had passed (the time according to her Series 10 Apple watch was 11:07 pm. Central) when Herb's phone rang. By that time Vielle had already stuffed the cash down in her purse and sent Herb's message to her father's prison-issue computer tablet. She was back on social media, on Instagram, watching a video an old friend had posted that showed a bunch of girls twerking to a Monaleo song outside of T's; a popular restaurant in the Fifth Ward' Kashmere Circle area. The video caused a nostalgic well of warmth to burgeon in her chest - but all that liquified Black Love turned ice cold when Herb's phone rung.

Vielle closed her eyes tight and tensed every muscle in her body, half-expecting the Bentley to blow like the Marriott had. But it didn't. Instead what she heard was the voice of a young woman with a notable Caribbean accent, a woman who sounded afraid and was doing her best to keep her voice down in spite of the Summer Walker melody that was blaring in the background.

"Hey, Uncle Theo. I was, uh … I was calling to see if you had, if you had cooked. Cooked dinner. I am *so* hungry."

Uncle Theo?"

Vielle turned her head and upper body to stare at the geriatric lunatic in the backseat. This time it was a look of concerned perplexity that wrinkled his brow, and there was maybe a two-second delay in his raspy response to the mystery woman's question.

"Yeah," he said, crushing his cigarette in the ashtray. "Meatloaf, mashed potatoes, corn, greens. Your plates in the microwave."

"Okay. I'll be over there soon, *really* soon, so leave the door unlocked.

I'd hate to have to ring the doorbell."

"I'll be woke. Love you."

Herb slipped the phone in his pocket and said, "Son of a bitch."

Vielle said, "what? What's wrong?"

"They made her. They know who she is." he thrust the straight end of his cane between the front seats, pointing at the house he'd been watching through his Nikons. "Pull up down there and park. This shit just got interesting."

Chapter 17

Black Reggie kept checking his rearview mirror, and his side mirror, and his Challenger's rearview camera, and looking back over his shoulder to peer around the side of his headrest.

No one back there now, but he'd seen them. He'd seen the headlights closing in behind him as he went roaring past the Lighthouse Mall. He'd done a bit of evasive maneuvering, careening onto Cedar Street before veering into the alleyway and pulling into some stranger's open car garage. He'd taken his .40-caliber Glock 23 out of the glove compartment and jacked the slide to chamber a round from the 10-shot clip, and he'd stood in the shadows of that garage for several heart-racing minutes, watching form beside a red and rusty tool chest as first a dark-colored Jaguar sedan went spending past on 8th Street and then, seconds later, a tan-colored Chevy Malibu.

Both of which he'd seen parked at the curb in front of Precious Tucker's house.

There were police cars streaking by in the opposite direction, too. Probably all on their way to that hotel fire everyone on Facebook was talking about. Reggie hadn't logged in to any social media accounts in weeks, but his girlfriend, Jasmeen Webb, was a Facebook fanatic (in-dire need of a Facebook intervention), and she'd called and told him all about the hotel fire that everyone on Facebook was talking about. People who lived near the hotel had reported hearing a big explosion. A gas leak was suspected.

Not that Black Reggie – or Reginald Fly, as his parents had christened him – gave three fucks about a goddamn hotel fire.

He backed out of the garage with his headlights off and crept down the pebble-strewn alley going no more than a few miles per hour, not even touching the gas pedal. His bloodshot eyes flitted in every direction. He was high out of his mind off promethazine and codeine and exotic weed, and therefore paranoid out of his mind, as well.

"Bitch-ass niggas got me fucked up," he said … quietly, under his breath. He braked near the mouth of the alley and was reaching back into the glove compartment, to grab his 30-round clip and switch it out with the standard 10-round mag, when another car he'd seen parked outside of Nubby's sister's house – a burgundy Dodge Charger with two broad white racing stripes – jetted past in front of him and slammed on the brakes.

An uncharacteristic bolt of fear thundered through Reggie at the sound of those tires screeching on the street. He saw the dim white glow of the Charger's reverse taillights, heard one excited black male voice urgently yelling something to someone else, but by then Reggie was already twisting around in his seat and speeding backward down the alley, the powerful vehicle's rear and wagging wildly from side to side.

"Not today, nigga. Not today," Reggie said.

A glance through his windshield showed him the Charger turning into the alley, and then he swung out onto Cedar with his front-end aimed at 9th Street and shot off like a bullet.

He made a left onto 10th Street and punched it. His hellcat engine responded in kind, taking the street and throwing it behind him in a blur. Adrenaline pounded through his veins like thoroughbred stallions at the Kentucky Derby. His heart felt as if a musclebound midget fairy all juiced up on steroids had flown in through a ventricle, got trapped inside and was now attempting to punch and kick his way back out.

A leftward-curving turn brought him out onto Michigan Boulevard. He slowed down at the very last second, made a sharp right turn, and slowed some more when he saw that an MCPD patrol car had pulled over the dark blue Jaguar half a block up.

Reggie's smartphone rang as he was riding past the Jag. He saw four young black men inside, young and thuggish in appearance, the flashing red and blue lights behind them illuminating the titanium scowls they regarded him with as he passed them by.

He answered the call without even checking to see who it was. The soft young female's voice that blossomed from eight of the Dodge's speakers sounded even more alarmed than Reggie felt.

"Nubby sent his boys to kill you! You need to go home. Fast. Like, *really* fast. I'm pretty sure Nubby's dead, but his boys don't know that. He put ten thousand dollars on your head, and everybody jumped in their cars and went looking for you."

That frightened voice belonged to Tonya Byrd, and Reggie didn't need to ask her to elaborate on her suspicion that Nubby might be dead. He'd known Markio for a long time, long enough to know that threatening him was worse than threatening the President.

"How many cars?" Reggie asked, checking his mirrors.

The answering voice belonged to Bambi Middlebrooks. "Four." And two seconds later: "Well actually it was three cars and a truck. A tan Malibu, a Charger with two big white lines up the middle ..."

Reggie's hearing seemed to shut down at that very moment, because the Charger with two big white lines up the middle had just appeared in his rearview mirror. It was slicing past the car dealership the Jaguar was pulled over next to, not speeding but certainly not cruising either, outpacing the other dozen or so motorists Reggie could see back there but only by four or five miles per hour.

Two uniformed policemen were walking up on the idling Jaguar with their flashlights beaming into the windows. Neither officer gave the passing Charger a first glance, let alone a second one.

" ... many gunshots," Bambi was saying. Sounded like a fuckin' *war* movie. Some John Wick-type shit. Soon as we turned the corner all you heard was *brrrrrrr*. I swear to God ..."

Reggie didn't stop at the Vail Street red light. He blew right through that motherfucker, because turning left toward the Walker Street house where he stored his stash of weed and weaponry would foolishly lead the enemy right to his doorstep. Markio was supposed to be meeting him there, but if Markio and his people weren't there yet, Reggie would be both outnumbered and outgunned, and that was a risk he was not willing to take.

The Michigan City Police Department stood elevated on a hill to his right the next block up. He sped past it as if its exterior surveillance cameras didn't work as well as he knew they did. Fuck the police. He'd take jail over hell any day.

Ejecting the 10-round magazine and inserting the thirty, he cast repeated glances at his rearview and side mirrors and drove on. Tonya and her two friends were still blabbing. Up ahead and across the oncoming traffic lane to Reggie's left, he saw that the BP gas station was alive with people, ten or eleven of them, milling sound beneath the well-lit canopy while someone played Cardi B's "Outside" from the open trunk of a late-eighties model Chevy Caprice.

Another check of the mirrors showed the Charger three car-lengths behind ... and closing in fast.

Reggie considered veering left and speeding onto the gas station platform, thinking that maybe all the cameras and witnesses would make his pursuers hesitant about coming after him, but then he remembered that there was ten thousand dollars on the line.

Those hoodlums would stop at nothing.

Which brought a bolder thought to Reggie's drug-addled mind: *What would Markio do?*

It came to him in an instant.

He ended the Bluetooth call, pressed the brake pedal to the floorboard, and spun the steering wheel to the right. His high-performance tires shrieked as the treads bit into the pavement, and when the car stopped at the yellow traffic light it was turned forty-five degrees to the right, with its passengers' side facing the Dodge Charger that had just swerved around a purple Ford Fusion to get behind him. He had just enough time to register the two faces behind the Charger's windshield - young black men with stone cold stares, just like the occupants of the pulled-over Jaguar - and then the doors were thrown open and the two men leapt out brandishing Draco pistols.

Black Reggie raised his gun and shot the passenger high in the chest of his white Armiri jogger. The switch at the back of Reggie's pistol made his gun shoot a dozen rounds in a single second, blasting through his passenger window and stitching a deadly pattern across the gunman's broad chest.

Then he was ducking and shoving his door open and diving into the street as the driver of the Charger opened fire, sending a barrage of 7.62 millimeter rounds through the passenger's side of the Challenger and rocking the $91,000 muscle car on its chassis.

Reggie lay flat on the street and didn't move for several infinite seconds. He squeezed his eyes shut and asked God for little help. Bits and pieces of glass rained down on the back of his neck. Then his car began to roll forward on its own, because he hadn't put the transmission in park nor engaged the emergency brake.

He popped open his eyes and rose up on his hands and knees, and then he popped up just as the back end of his car deserted him and took aim at the tall skinny man-child who for some reason was still shooting into the Challenger. He was swinging his Draco back in Reggie's direction when

Reggie let off another one-second burst that emptied his clip completely.

The gunman's left shoulder jerked backward, and he fell to the ground next to his open-door. His Draco went skittering away from him, rotating like a fidget spinner, and was promptly run over by a large white man in a small white Volkswagen who, along with four other wise motorists, went speeding around the crime scene and through the red traffic light.

Someone at the BP yelled, *"That's Black Reggie! Santana! Santana, look, that's Reggie!"*

The shout snapped Reggie back to his senses. He was standing in the middle of a relatively busy intersection, holding a de-cocked pistol and eyeing the grounded figures of a burly dead man and a scrawny wounded man while his bullet-riddled Dodge Challenger Hellcat jumped the curb and slowed to a stop.

He turned and ran toward the gas station, feeling the blood trickle down from his kneecaps and the palm of his left hand, from when he'd kneeled in the glass. He'd left his phone in the car. He'd left an open pint of Wackhardt syrup and a baggie with about a quarter ounce of exotic wee in it snuggled in one of his cupholders. But he was alive.

He had just made it under the BP canopy and was looking back over his shoulder when he saw that the pink boys who'd pulled over the Jaguar were now back in their squad car and racing toward the scene of the shooting, their blue-and-reds flashing like titties at Mardi Gras.

Several vehicles had sped off from the gas station, but three of them remained. One was Santana's clean gray Infiniti SUV. Another was Marlene Eckwood's canary yellow Toyota Camry.

The third vehicle was a burnt orange Range Rover on big gold rims. Its driver's window was all the way down, its front end parked close to the building. Reggie glimpsed a bit of movement in the driver's side mirror, but his eyes didn't linger long enough to see anything more.

"Get in, nigga!" Santana said, jumping into the passenger's seat of his truck while his girlfriend, a pretty yellow woman named Sky, got in the driver's seat and shifted into drive.

Santana was a short brown man, shirtless and wearing white cotton Chrome Hearts shorts with gray and blue crosses patched all over them. A ghostly serpentine scar slithered up from just below his navel to the center of his chest, a chilling reminder of the ice pick he'd taken to the gut in a club brawl two decades ago.

As soon as Reggie was in the back seat with the door closed he got to work removing the metal switch from the back of his Glock. Sky drove them off the platform and onto School Street, which ran alongside the gas station. There was a slight incline of maybe twenty-two degrees where School intersected with Holiday Street; Reggie glanced back down that low hill and saw the patrol car arrive at the scene of the shooting.

He also saw the front end of that burnt orange Range Rover, peeking out from the side of the BP as if it wanted to pursue the fleeing Infiniti truck. Only it didn't it stayed there. Idling. Watching.

"Boy, on David, I ain't know you had that in you," Santana said. *Boy* came out *boa*. Santana was a Black Disciple from the notorious Low End neighborhood on Chicago's South Side. He was used to the adrenaline-fueled thrill of gun violence; Reggie was not. "Folks, you good back there?"

Black Reggie shook his dark bald head from side to side. He wasn't good at all.

Chapter 18

Officer Kolita Pierre had viewed the text message on Loochie's phone screen from the corner of her eye as she sat on his lap on his cranberry-colored living room sofa.

Ay, keep that Haitian girl with you until I get there. Just found out she the opps.

Loochie had immediately snatched the phone back to his hip, to get it out of her line of vision, but he was too late. She'd already seen it. Thirty seconds later Kolita got up and walked out of the living room into the kitchen and out the back door. A short walk through a nice house. She'd phoned Herb as she went, pausing to speak with him on the concrete walkway that began outside the back door and wrapped around to the driveway.

There were only a few people inside the house. Everyone else - six men and five women, not including Kolita - was in the backyard, drinking beers and cups of tequila, watching the sky over the tall wooden fence that separated them from Southgate Apartments.

Thick black clouds of smoke swirled up into the heavens from the Marriott hotel three-quarters of a mile away.

Chris Brown's "Residuals" was playing, but only one of the girls seemed to be enjoying it. The others were talking about the earthshaking blast that had shaken them all to silence forty-eight minutes earlier.

Kolita was not surprised to hear Loochie walking up behind her even before she ended her brief conversation with

Herb. She had expected it. She'd had her purse open and her gun within easy reach in anticipation of it.

"Who was that?" Loochie asked.

Kolita beamed a fictitious smile. "My crazy-ass uncle Theo. I was seeing if he'd cooked dinner."

"Did he?"

"Mm hm. I'm about to head over there to eat before I … Shit, I guess I'll have to find another hotel, huh?" She giggled, as cheery as a cheerio. "I mean, now that the Marriott's all blown up."

"Yeah, I guess so."

Loochie wasn't smiling. His expression was as hard and smooth as a stone that had been rolling along a riverbed for a few thousand years. He was tall and brown, handsome and skinny, a good-looking skeleton with peanut butter bones. He had a blunt wedged behind his right ear. His phone was in his bony right hand, a call running on the screen. Kolita didn't have to ask to know who was on the other end of that call.

"Who you think blew that hotel up?" Loochie looked at the rising black smoke dragons in the distance. "Think it was that old man? The one who killed them two brothers in Chicago last week?"

Kolita shrugged and turned so that Loochie was facing her instead of standing behind her right shoulder. "I was thinking it might've been a gas leak at first, but … I don't know. I'm just glad I wasn't there. Glad I was here with you and your people."

The razor-sharp spike of horror that almost seemed to skewer her body to the ground at that moment was very real indeed, nothing like the prosthetic smile she'd worn a moment prior. What if she *had* been there at that hotel? Would Herb have killed her too?

She had spoken with Titus about it. He'd called her in a panic maybe two minutes after the deadly blast. He was at the Buffalo Wild Wings just up the road from the Marriott, dining with a woman named Crystal who swore she'd known Millionaire Markio for years, when the not-so-distant explosion rocked the whole world around him, rattling window panes and setting off dozens of car alarms in the parking lot out front. When he went outside and saw the fire and smoke billowing out of the hotel down the street, he'd instantly known.

"He's gonna kill us, Pierre," he'd said. "He's gonna kill us all. There's no big bag of money at the end of this. That black son of a bitch probably hates cops. What the fuck were we thinking?"

There was never any assumption that Rice, Austin, Meredith, and the former Lieutenant Storms weren't there at the Marriott. Titus had gotten a text from Austin not even twenty minutes before the boom saying they were gathered there to meet with Herb, and Kolita had been on the phone with Rice while Austin's busy little thumbs were working on that text message.

Kolita shivered and scissored her legs one over the other, as if she had to pee. A lightning bug flitted past in her periphery, its tail end blinking a bright yellow morse code to its firefly associates, who blinked their tails in return. A warm eddy of a breeze blew through the yard, carrying with it the harsh stench of smoke and burned plastics ... and maybe other things that had been burned.

"Twelve confirmed dead so far," said one of Loochie's female friends as she crossed the yard to join them by the screen door. She'd introduced herself as Chop, and she was brown like Loochie and pretty in an ordinary sort of way. She held up her phone to show them the news article she'd been reading. "See? It's right here on CNN." Then, in an utterly incredulous tone of voice: "On *CNN!* Ain't that some shit? They done put Michigan City on CNN. that shit ain't happened since Alexus and Bulletface lived out here. We should drive over there and talk to the camera people. Get on TV."

Loochie shook his head and pushed his bottom lip out an inch. Kolita watched the long-faced man who'd introduced himself as Mark B walk over with an ice-cold Bud Light in one hand and a Samsung phone in the other. He was about five inches shorter than Loochie and had more meat on his bones.

"They say some niggas just got killed on the west side too," he said. "Right across from the Center. Sherri Crump said she was on her front porch smokin' a cigarette when two black trucks whipped up on Precious and her people three houses down. Like ten niggas jumped out, fully automatics. Say they shot Precious, killed her brother Nubby, and killed three *mo'* mothafuckas."

Chop said, "I heard Markio was the one who shot Julius earlier today, and you know that was Nubby's son."

"And look at this shit." Mark B turned his phone so they could all see the screen. Someone named Marlene Eckwood had just shared a Facebook Live video of a huge police presence at the intersection of a wide four-lane street. There was a body under a crisp white sheet next to a red Dodge Charger with white racing stripes on the hood, roof, and trunk. "That's right in front of the Duke, right by the police station. Marlene say them niggas shot at Black Reggie, shot his whole car up, but that nigga hopped out and shot back and hit both'a them niggas."

Chop sucked a tooth. Kolita thought she looked like a cross between Rihanna Fenty and Solange Knowles. She wore a small pink tee over tight blue jeans and pink Reebok Classics. "The Duke is a gas station on Michigan Boulevard," she said to Kolita. "It used to be Duke of Oil, now it's a BP, but a lot of us still call it the Duke."

Kolita nodded, said, "The Duke," and thought, *I need to get the fuck outta here before Markio show up.*

"Shit always go down at the Duke," Mark B confided. "Used to be like that at the game room, too. That was before they tore down Harbor Side projects."

Kolita snatched a glance at her diamond watch. "My Uber should be pulling up in a minute. I gotta get to my uncle's house."

"Where he live at?" Loochie asked. The call time on his phone screen was still rolling along, five minutes fifty seconds and counting.

"Not far from here." Kolita began walking toward the driveway, waving goodbye to Loochie's guests, consulting the Uber app on her phone. She had a new text message from Titus. He was already on Interstate 94, on his way back to Chicago. The bastard had left her behind, like an unwanted child in a crowded mall.

She was walking along the passenger's side of someone's bronze-colored Acura sedan when Loochie's long bony fingers closed around the nape of her neck. An attempt at reaching into her purse got it ripped loose from her shoulder. Her chest thumped against the Acura's rear passenger's side window, and she winced as Loochie squeezed.

"You know you done fucked up, right?" Loochie said, quoting the bald brown detective from *Menace to Society*.

"Let me go."

"Aw, I'ma let you go. Soon's my nigga get here."

"I'm a cop." Kolita tried to twist free of Loochie's grip on her neck, but his fingers were like steel cables. She could hardly breathe. "I am an officer with the Chicago Police Department. If you … give me a second … I'll prove it."

"Yeah, yeah, yeah. Michale Jordan's my long-lost brother. Fuck outta here."

"Either you let go of me right now or I'll arrest you for assault on a public safety officer, obstructing a cross-state federal investigation, attempted murder by way of strangulation, attempted rape, attempted sodomy …"

Loochie's fingers loosened quite a bit. "Attempted murder? Rape? Ain't nobody tried to rape you, kill you. Fuck kinda shit you on?"

129

"The kinda shit that'll get you two-life sentences if you don't get your hand off the back of my neck."

He let go of her, and in that same instant she heard a vicious *wish-wish* sound that reminded her of a whip lashing through the air. She spun around fast, not sure what she would do when she faced him but sure she would do something.

What stopped her was the sight of his left hand, the hand he'd grabbed her with. The entire top half of it was gone. All four fingers and the upper part of his palm lay dead and bleeding on the smooth gray concrete between his blue-and-white Jordan sneakers. The half of a hand he still had attached to his wrist squirted hot red blood onto Kolita's neck and chin. His eyes became double zeros, his mouth trembled open, and his head turned slowly to look at the jet black octogenarian who was standing a foot and a half to his left.

The old man had appeared out of thin air, it seemed. Kolita certainly hadn't seen him. Not until now. He had his head tilted forwards in a supremely sinister grin. In his right hand he held the blonde wood handle of his cane, only instead of being attached to the straight end of darker wood it had become the grip for an eighteen to twenty-inch sword.

"Need a hand?" Herb asked in his snakishly hissing rasp.

Loochie uttered a choked cry and fell over sideways, landing hard on the driveway; the taller they are, the harder they fall. The only part of him that didn't fall was the lower part of his left leg, from mid-calf down to his shoe. That part of him remained standing, because it was no longer attached to the rest of him. The impossibly sharp blade of Herb's cane sword had sliced right through it, bone and all. It looked like an oversized sushi roll that had been doused in blood and stuffed down in a white sock which had then been stuffed in a Jordan shoe.

"My *hand!*" Loochie cried. "My *leg!* You cut off my shit! You cut off my shit!" He raised himself up on an elbow and turned to scream for his boys in the backyard. *"Beezy! BEEZY! Smoke! This nigga cut …"*

He was still yelling for his crew when Herb and Kolita got in the backseat of Herb's shining black Mulsanne. No one heard Loochie's cries for help until he'd dragged himself into the backyard, because Chris Brown's "Residuals" had segued into Chief Keef's "Faneto," and everyone had started rapping along to the lyrics.

By the time Loochie's associates realized that two of his limbs had been shortened, and that there was strawberry jam gushing out of those cleanly severed peanut butter sticks, Herb's $300, 000 Bentley was gone from their street.

Chapter 19

"Hm. back so soon?"

Markio stopped outside his bedroom door and smiled at the glorious warmth he felt in his heart. He hadn't even crossed the threshold and already he was under her droopy-eyed spell.

Morena was sitting up in bed with the TV remote in one hand, a bowl of popcorn on her lap, and the little black dog nestled close to her hip. *Top Five* was playing on the huge widescreen television. The movie was at the point where Chris Rock's character had just met Rosario Dawson'. The two of them were walking shoulder to shoulder on the sidewalk, smiling and talking and basking in the sunshine.

Morena paused the movie as Markio stepped into the room.

"I see you done got all comfortable in my bed," he said.

"I wasn't sure which room you wanted me to take in that guest house, there were clothes and bags in a few of them, and I didn't know how late you'd be getting in, so I figured I'd -"

"No-no-no-no-no," Markio said quickly. "You stay right there. I need you in here with me anyway. What if I choke to death in my sleep? Have a seizure or some'n? What good it's gon' do to have a nurse in my guest house when I'm choking to death in the main house."

Morena tipped her head back in laughter and then rolled her bloodshot eyes behind their droopy lids. She was wearing a white pair of Gucci yoga shorts that seemed to have been vacuum-sealed to her meaty thighs and a small matching tee. Her feet were pretty, the nails pedicured and painted dark purple like her fingernails. The room smelled like weed smoke, and the evidence was in the previously empty Louis Vuitton ashtray on his bedside table. She'd smoke her blunt down to the roach.

"You're funny," she said.

"I'm serious," Markio shifted his gaze to the dog. "And you - you fuckin' traitor. That's all it took was some popcorn and a thick thigh, nigga?"

Chief Sosa whined and lowered his head next to the thick thigh in question, covering his eyes with his front right paw. The capitulating gesture elicited a second burst of magical laughter from the angel in Markio's bed, and the laugh made Markio chuckle.

He went into his giant walk-in closet and through the doorway in the back wall that opened into his massive gray marble bathroom. Two m minutes later he was naked in the shower, scrubbing himself clean with the helpful aid of a gold mesh loofah and foamy white curds of Dove body wash, not thinking of the banana-hued beauty in his bed but of the pear-shaped head he'd emptied Keanan's gun into - and also the bloodcurdling scream he'd heard from his good friend Loochie.

My hand! My leg! You cut off my shit! You cut off my shit!

Markio wasn't surprised to learn that Herb had been waiting near Loochie's house for him to arrive. Nor was he shocked by what assuredly had to be a sword attack, with the blade drawn from within the length of the old man's cane. That was Herb's modus operandi. He'd done the same thing to Weezy, the former owner of the most popular strip club in all of Chicago. Lopped Weezy's right hand off at the wrist. Months later he'd planted a bomb under the promising young entrepreneur's sports car and blasted him into a thousand and one pieces. The FBI's final conclusion was that roughly three and a half pounds of C4-explosive had been used in the car bomb that killed Roy "Weezy" Sullivan, and Markio was willing to bet that the same type of explosive was used in the Marriott Hotel bombing.

The only question was why, and the only answer Markio could think of was that Herb had bombed the hotel to cover up something. Either that or he'd done it as a distraction, but Markio didn't think that was the case. A cover-up was the most logical deduction. Maybe Herb had been staying there ever since he killed the Slauson brothers last week and learned from Jacobi that Markio was lying low somewhere in Michigan City, and maybe someone had recognized Herb's face from the news. Or maybe he'd killed off the men who'd accompanied him and the Haitian girl to the Lincoln Park mansion. *Yeah*, Markio thought. *That's probably it right there. They knew too much. They died because they knew too much about the most wanted man in America.*

"Everybody else who died was just collateral damage," Markio muttered aloud to himself." wrong place at the wrong time."

A tiny giggle alerted him to Morena's presence. He could tell from the close proximity of sound that she was either standing in the bathroom doorway or lingering just beyond it.

"Wrong place at the wrong time," she echoed mockingly. "What the hell? Are you in here talking to yourself? You do know they have medication for things like that, right?"

"Ay, maaan," Markio said, his smile coming through in his voice. "I ain't hire you to eavesdrop on me … on my personal monologues."

"Oh, is that what that was? A monologue? You think you're the black Stephen Colbert?"

Markio laughed. "You got me fucked up." He shut off the water. "I was thinkin' out loud. Thinkin' about that hotel blast. Herb did that shit to cover some'n up. Everybody else who died was just at the wrong place at the wrong time."

Morena didn't reply. Markio took a thick gray Louis Vuitton bath towel from outside the glass shower door and began rubbing himself dry. For a minute he thought Morena had returned to the bedroom to finish her movie. Then she said, "Says here on CNN that the FBI's already en route, and the death toll's up to nineteen now. The hotel clerk reported seeing someone who matches Herbert's description leaving out right before the explosion." In a lower tone she added, "This is soooo sad. All those innocent people. How could someone ...?"

She didn't finish the question, and she didn't need to. Markio could fill the blank. How could someone *be so evil*? How could someone *intentionally kill so many innocent people*? There were perhaps a hundred thousand ways to end that daunting question, but Markio couldn't think of a single answer to either of them.

He lotioned his skin with Jergens and deodorized his armpits with Right Guard gel after pulling on his Calvin Klein boxer briefs and a black pair of Dior shorts he sometimes used as pajamas.

Morena was exploring his sneaker collection when he returned to his closet. "I wish I'd have known that was a bathroom," she said, picking a yellow and white Fendi sneaker off the second shelf and giving it a perfunctory sniff. "I had to pee so bad like twenty minutes ago. I went way down to the end of the hall and used that one."

"She got a bathroom in every bedroom." Markio sat down on the gray leather upholstered-bench and placed the bottle of Jergens next to his hip.

"She?"

"Yeah, she. Alexus Costilla. This her mansion. She just asked me to stay here awhile, until that whole shit with Herb died down."

"Wow." Morena put the shoe back where she got it. "You know what? I do remember you now. Alexus posted a pic with you on her Instagram a few years back. Something about your books. You had started dating her friend, that lawyer."

"Nikkia Staples."

"Yeah. Yeah, that's her name." A thoughtful smirk stole across Morena's strikingly pallid pink lips. "Man, you're so lucky to know people like them. Alexus is worth, what, four hundred billion dollars?"

"Some'n like that. Here, rub some of this on my back." He proffered the bottle of Jergens.

"You want a massage?" Her eyes widened by maybe half a centimeter as she took the bottle. "I'm really good at giving massages. I kind of have to be. When you work with patients who have muscular dystrophy, multiple sclerosis, things like that, you have to know how to massage away those muscle aches. You need to lie down i n bed, on your stomach, with your head at the foot of the bed. Come on."

Markio had only meant for her to rub a little lotion on his back, but he wasn't about to argue against a massage. He put on a fresh pair of socks, noting while he pulled them on that the cash he'd gotten from Slime was now stacked neatly on top of his glass jewelry display case. He didn't mention it, but witnessing Morena's penchant for cleanliness definitely left an impression.

He got up and preceded her back out to the bedroom. He'd dropped his phone in his pocket when he put on the shorts, and he brought it back out as he and Morena climbed onto the bed.

"Why did you keep sending me to voicemail?" Morena squeezed a nickel-sized amount of lotion into her hand as she kneeled next to him. As soon as he buried his chin in the gray silk pillow he took from in front of the headboard, she mounted him with her knees flanking his waist and said, "I called you once right after your family left, and I called you again after I got off the phone with Brittany."

"I left my phone down there in the garage before I left. We all did."

136

"So the police couldn't use the cell towers to track you all to and from wherever you went."

Markio shrugged because it was true. He hadn't spoken with Loochie until he was back at the mansion, sitting in his snow white Bugatti Veyron in the six-car garage with Slime in the passenger seat next to him. He was in the process of backing out of the garage to race to Loochie's south side home – it would have taken him no more than four or five minutes to get there in the Bugatti – when the Haitian woman issued her threat of a bogus arrest. Seconds later he heard Herb's gritty old voice, the voice of a man who'd smoked so many unfiltered Pall malls over the past eight decades that he had several strands of DNA made entirely of tobacco. *Need a hand?*

All the Earls had gone back home to Chicago. They all had their own lives to deal with, children and spouses, mortgages and careers. The Fin Ball Shortiez had wanted to stay, but Markio didn't want his two Escalades on the property so soon after the west side shooting, so they too were gone. Besides the round-the-clock security detail of seven armed men who were outside patrolling the property on foot, only Markio and Morena remained.

Daubing the lotion across the surface of his upper back, where the word ALMIGHTY was inked in large cursive lettering, Morena said, "What's the meaning behind this tattoo?"

"Some gang shit. I'm a Traveler, you know, a TVL, but all branches of Vice Lord fall under the Almighty umbrella. Same with the Four Corner Hustlers, the Black P. Stones, the Latin Kings, and even some of the Bloods. We all got that five-pointed star as our primary gang symbol. It represents the five highest principles known to man: Love, Truth, Peace, Freedom, and Justice."

"Oh." Morena was massaging the part of his back that was just below his neck. "So it's like one big brotherhood."

"In prison it is. Not so much on the streets. Nigga's got their own cliques out here, their own gangs. In the joint all the different branches of Vice Lord - Travelers, Conservatives, Unknowns, Mafia Insane, Cicero Insanes, Imperial Insanes, Undertakeres - we all come together as the AVLN, the Almighty Vice Lord Nations I was always a high-ranking member, an elite, so I gave a lot of orders, got some people fucked around for disrespectin' the mob, got some of the bros beat up for violatin' laws and principles. Made sure the money was right. It was hard work, managing a bunch of criminals, but I think I did a pretty good job. My main goal was to cut down that recidivism rate. Education was paramount. I *forced* niggas to go to school, to get their diplomas and GED's and college degrees, to spend their time constructively so that, upon their release, they could uplift and contribute to the same communities they came from."

"And you still do that?"

"Hell no." Well … I … Shit, I don't know. I'll be honest, I was one foot in and one foot out for a long time, but that part of my life is over. I'm a writer now, a professional, Oscar-nominated screenwriter. As of today I'm officially retiring from the streets. First thing tomorrow I'ma charter us a private jet to the Bahamas, get us the fuck away from here. I see I gotta cut ties to my own city for a while. You know it's time to go when you got the Chicago Police Department workin' side by side with a wanted killer just to get you out the way."

"You're saying Herbert Harris has the police working *with* him?"

Markio nodded his chin in the pillow. "All day I've been tryna remember where I knew that Haitian girl from." He lifted his iPhone and went to a thread of text messages between him and Big Gabby, an old friend of his with whom he'd gone into business a year and a half ago. Together they'd founded Merrihill Equity Group, a conglomerate of seven young Black millionaires that purchased struggling businesses, transformed them into upscale companies, and split the monthly profits. One of those businesses was Weezy's old strip joint, Queen of Diamonds, and it was there, from the upstairs VIP Lounge, where Markio had seen CPD Officer Kolita Pierre.

The video Big Gabby had sent to him was an overhead view of three Chicago police officers entering the blue-carpeted vestibule just inside the front doors of QOD. Morena gasped when she saw the Haitian woman in uniform.

"I was in the VIP Lounge with Alexus and Princess, lookin' down from behind the glass, when these three cops walked in. They were there to arrest Blicky Nicky for splittin' Shmoney Rose's head with that bottle. Happened in my section too. I had front row seats to that shit."

"I saw that on *The Real Baddies of Chicago*," Morena said, using her fingertips to press and knead the muscles in the back of his left shoulder. "I'm not really into reality TV, but I did see that episode. And now that you mention it, I think I do remember seeing you and all your boys sitting there when that fight went down. Everybody had on those big FBS chains."

"That was us." Three words submerged in a lake of pride. "I bought all them chains. We were twenty deep in VIP that night. Had twenty guns on us too. I remember being nervous about it when I saw these cops walk in. I watched this Pierre chick walk from the front of the club all the way to the doorway Cherish Taylor was standing in."

"I'm lost. Why would a Chicago police officer be in Michigan City, Indiana? That's out of their - what's that word?"

"Jurisdiction."

"Yeah, that's it. This isn't their jurisdiction."

"Herb paid her to come out here and find me. That's all it is. Same with Whitney. She sent that nigga Pudgy at me, prob'ly offered him a bankroll to catch me at that mall and shoot up my car. My nigga Fat Jeremy told me she used to fuck with Pudgy around the time I blew his hand off. If he left the hospital today and went straight to Chicago, it was to see her. I guarantee it."

"When I talked to Brittany, she told me that the man who was shot in his thumb earlier today was just killed somewhere on the west side. Him and like three other people. His sister was shot too. One of Amanda's friends was dating the guy you shot –"

"Ay, maaan," Markio interjected, like an overzealous preacher.

Morena snickered once. "You know what I mean."

"No the fuck I don't." "Whatever. Anyway, what I was about to say was, the boy who shot at your car, he was a Vice Lord too. So was his father and all his brothers and cousins. Why would they accept someone's money to go after you when you're all essentially on the same team? I thought you guys were supposed to like each other."

"Man, fuck them niggas. I don't give a fuck what gang they in. Almighty don't like nobody. You play, you lay – simple as that."

"That is so crazy."

"No, it ain't." With a grunt and a twist, Markio rolled over on his back. Almost unconsciously, he began rubbing his hands up and down Morena's thighs, from her knees to her hips and back don to her knees. "Look at it like this. Let's say a cop walks into a police station and opens fire on his own fellow officers. Are they wrong if they shoot back and kill him?"

Morena had no comeback for that. She merely sat there staring down at him in the semi dark room. He kept rubbing at her thighs, softly and soothingly, for the moment ignoring the growing length of muscle in his shorts. Morena's nipples were hard as stone behind the fabric of her shirt. Her tea brown eyes traced the outline of Markio's lips, then moved down to the Chicago Bulls logo tattooed on his left pectoral muscle, and the big CUP GANG tattoo that covered most of his stomach, and then her eyes went down a bit further, to gauge the size and shape of the lead pip he was concealing in his briefs.

"I, uh … I don't … you know," she said. "Not on the first night."

Markio didn't agree or disagree. What he did was scoot and wriggle under Morena, moving himself toward the center of the bed until the plump print of her labia was practically resting on his chin. Then he grabbed hold of her thighs and began to lick and suck her pussy right through her skintight Gucci shorts.

She gasped. "Oouu, you … ooouuu, you slick fucker, you slick sonofabitch," she said, taking in deep tremulous breaths and throwing them out just as shakily.

Markio thought her sex smelled like some exotic forbidden fruit that had yet to be discovered. He could taste the sweetness of her juices through the fabric. He flared his nostrils, inhaling as much of that wonderful scent as his lungs could take.

"Boy … you gon' make me come … all in these shorts … Markio … *Mmm, Markio!*"

He liked the way she said his name. Her naturally sexy voice was enhanced by a sultry inflection of ecstasy. He curled his fingers behind the waistband of her shorts, intent on yanking them down, but Morene beat him to the punch, raking them off with her thumbs and kicking them over the foot of the bed. She sat astride his mouth with her feet next to his ears and rocked her hips back and forth, palming the waves on the top of his head in one small delicate hand while splaying the fingers of her other hand on the bed for balance. There was a large square mirror affixed to the ceiling directly over the bed, offering an ethereal view of the two of them from above, but Markio only caught a glimpse of it. His sole focus was on Morena; not her reflection, but the gorgeous woman herself.

It wasn't long before his chin and the outside of his mouth were slick with her delectable juices. That Bruno Mars song, "Fat, Juicy, and Wet", could easily have been written about Morena Manfield. Her pussy was like a skinless peach on Markio's tongue, soft and sweet and incredibly delicious, and he sucked on it like a man who hadn't had food or water in days, sucked on her rigid clitoris like an infant at his mother's breast.

For a while the only sounds to be heard were the ecstatic yelps of Morena's pornographic moans and the wet slurping noises from the face she was sitting on. Markio's dick was a stone serpent, pulsating in his CK boxer-briefs. On his way up from the garage he'd received a text from Black Reggie's girlfriend saying he'd just been arrested for a murder and an attempted murder – *They snatched him outta Santana's truck*, the text had read – but that was the furthest thing from Markio's mind. He wanted to make Morena come and then fuck her until he idd the same. Everything else would have to wait.

The former want was achieved in exactly five minutes and fifty seconds. "Herre i come. Here I come. Here I come,' Morena said, speaking between moans. "Here I *Come!*"

Markio applied a firmer grip on her thighs as Morena's curvy body began to twitch and tremble. The orgasm dropped the full weight of her onto his smiling mouth. The steady flow of her sugary vaginal juices doubled, tripled, until Markio had to lift her off his mouth to keep from drowning in it. He licked his lips and swallowed, grinning triumphantly as he watched her fleshy pink pussy petals quiver and drip through a tense series of orgasmic contractions that made her ass and thighs bounce and jiggle.

Such a beautiful thing to behold.

"Whoa." Morena snickered. "You are *good* at that. *Man.*"

Markio was contemplating a witty remark when he glimpsed a dark blot of movement in the ceiling mirror. He turned his head just in time to see Chief go bounding out of the bedroom with Morena's yoga shorts clenched between his teeth.

"Hey!" Morena shouted. "Sosa! No! *Bad* dog! Those are *mine*!"

She jumped out of bed and Chief Sosa took flight, his paws clicking on the marble-tiled floor as he made his getaway with her yoga shorts dragging beside him.

Markio cracked up laughing. He sat up, rose up on his knees, and laughed some more when Morena turned to look at him.

"If you don't go out there and get my shorts back from that dog," she said, an incomplete sentence that in the black community suggested a threat.

"Man, fuck them shorts. I'll buy you some more shorts. Get over here." He thumbed down the front of his own shorts and the boxer-briefs he wore beneath them. His dick flopped out in front of him, a long veiny appendage that was at least five shades darker than the rest of his skin.

Morena's mouth dropped open and her eyebrows went up. There was no droop to her eyelids now; the whites of her eyes were still congested with crimson veins, but the lids were so far apart that they seemed to be missing altogether.

"Boy, what did you … how did it …" She drifted off, still staring. Chief Sosa reappeared in the doorway, his tail wagging merrily, Morena's brand-new yoga shorts handing down from his canine mouth, but now she paid him no mind. She couldn't take her eyes off Markio's magic stick. "I didn't think it'd be so *big*." she mouthed something else, but Markio didn't catch what it was.

He opened the second drawer in his nightstand, flicked aside the two paperbacks he'd been reading – Jaquavis Coleman's *The Streets Have No King* and Malcolm Gladwell's *Outliers* – and reached to the back for his stash of extra-large Magnum condoms.

Morena climbed back onto the bed. She kneeled with her back to him and spread her knees apart as she bent forward on her hands, arched her back, and craned her neck to look back at him.

"Don't try to slide it all in at once," she said, and was that worry in her eyes? Certainly looked like it. "I think I can take the girth, but I've never been with a man whose dick was as long as yours."

"You'll be good." Markio was biting his bottom lip and grinning as he moved in behind her. "I ain't gon' hurt you too much. I know how to fuck." .

He tore open the gold wrapper and rolled the lubricated rubber down the impressive length of his erection. His eyes traversed the soft yellow slopes of Morena's ass. He gave each cheek a sharp, meaningful slap and took a generous moment to admire the ensuing jiggles. Then he moved closer and slowly guided himself into her.

Gang members fuck way better than ordinary nine-to-fivers. It's a scientifically proven fact. There's more aggression in every deeply penetrating thrust, more animosity in every skin clapping stroke. Add to that the two Percocets Markio had taken - one before going on the drill and the other immediately after - and Morena was in serious trouble.

"You ain't even ready," he said, under his breath.

Morena moaned in reply and reached under her belly and between her parted thighs to fiddle with her distended clitoris, while Markio placed his scarred brown hands on the sides of her narrow waist and began sliding his dick in and out of her. He didn't take it slow, but he didn't necessarily go fast either. Not initially. He took his time, enjoying the warm, wet feel of Morena's tightly gripping vaginal walls, gradually increasing the pace of his thrusts and occasionally halting to smack and rub on her ass before starting up again.

Five minutes passed. Then ten. Then twenty. Millionaire Markio was like the Energizer Bunny with all the oxycodone he had coursing through his bloodstream. Morena's moans sync perfectly with the incessant clasp of Markio's pelvis against her ass and the slashing sounds of her sopping wet ladyhole.

One hour and four positions later, Markio dug in deep and shot off into the condom, filling it with a load of semen so heavy that it made the end of the rubber sag low on his cockhead.

Morena was positioned doggystyle with the side of her face sunken into the middle of the bed when it happened. By then she had moaned and quivered her way through three more orgasms. Markio got up and went to flush the condom, and when he returned to find Morena folded in the exact same position he laughed and smacked her on the ass. Then he leaned in to give her swollen, defeated pussy a loud, wet kiss.

"There you go. That's all you needed right there," he said, falling back onto the bed beside her.

"Oh my Lord." Morena snickered breathlessly, but she still didn't move. "Girlfriend had it right. That really was some superdick. My ex, his dick is like a little white shrimp. Matt Johnston. He's a military boy, just twenty-four years old, no idea what to do with all this black girl ass. *You*, though – you got it right."

Finally she rose up on her knees and turned to him with a weak smile on her face and her hand raised for a high five. Markio met her hand in the middle. After that she excused herself to the bathroom and journeyed there on shaky legs. Watching the rise and fall of her meaty buttocks over the toes of his socks, Markio thought he had the best view on Beachwalk Lane.

He picked up the remote and flipped to MTN News. a caramel-skinned news reporter named Tiffany Roscoe had already made the forty-minute drive from Chicago to Michigan City. She was just one of a dozen news reporters standing in front of their respective network's cameras, across the road from the smoldering building. All of them were speaking in serious, dramatic tones. The kind of histrionic reporting that would have viewers clinging to their every word.

"Herbert Harris was last seen leaving this Marriott hotel mere seconds before the blast. Authorities believe he may have triggered the explosion from inside his car, a black Bentley Mulsanne with Illinois license plate …"

Morena came out wearing a white pair of Dior sweatpants that Markio had purchased for himself during a weekend he'd spent with adult film star Yasmine. "BunnyXXX" Gordon at the St. Regis Bal Harbour Resort in Miami Beach, Florida.

The sweatpants looked better on Morena than they ever would on him.

"I knew it was Herb," he said and pointed at the TV. "He been driving that Bentley for the past couple years. I can't believe it took them this long to figure it out."

"You should have called the FBI and told them what kind of car he drove." Morena climbed onto the bed and slipped beneath the covers, so Markio followed suit. "And you shut off my movie."

"I don't call no police. If I dial nine-one-one it's gon' be for a heart attack or a house fire. All that other shit for the birds."

"But he's kind of a terrorist. It's not snitching if you call the police on a terrorist."

"I don't call no police," Markio repeated, and this time there was a note of finality in his words. He handed her the remote and stared up at the ceiling mirror. His reflection grinned back at him.

"You think he knows about you living here?"

The man on the ceiling shook his head. "Nah. Most of my family didn't even know until tonight. If he knows where I live, he got that information directly from Alexus."

Just the mention of the world's wealthiest woman summoned a smile from Morena that was so radiant it seemed the skin on her face was wrapped around a star. She held the remote to her chin but didn't switch back to her movie. After some time she asked, "How much do you think she makes off MTN?"

"Alexus? Shit, I don't know. Billions, obviously. She got the Minority Television channel, then the streaming app, then MTN News, MTN Films, MTN Studios. That four hundred billion she got came from a lot of different businesses outside of MTN, too. She got oil refineries, stocks and bonds, a luxury real estate business. All kinda shit."

Markio didn't add that Alexus and the rest of the Costilla clan also ran the Matamoros drug cartel. Half the world had seen Alexus and her family go to trial for allegedly heading the notorious Mexican cartel. Since her acquittal, Queen A had distanced herself from her paternal family and their Matamoras associates, but she was still very much in charge of the drug cartel itself, a global narco-trafficking organization that had made her a whole lot more than four hundred billion dollars. Markio wouldn't have been surprised to learn that Queen A had actually shot past the billionaire girls club to become the world's first trillionaire.

"Herb actually got rich because of his dealings with Alexus' father," Markio said, looking at his reflection but talking to Morena. "This was back in the eighties, the late eighties, I might've been two years old. Herb used to do business with Papi Costilla, for Jeff Fort and the Black P. Stones. He would drive down to Mexico to make the deals. My mama told me about that shit twenty years ago."

"I don't understand. How did he get rich from middlemanning deals? What were they, drug deals?"

"I don't know, might've been. It wasn't the middleman deals that got him rich. Jeff was already in the feds by then, and Herb was just doing him a favor. What got Herb rich was what he learned from papi. See, back in eighty-eight, this mathematics professor named Jim Simons figured out a way to beat the stock market. He created the Medallion Fund, and every year for thirty years straight it increased whatever you invested by sixty-six percent. If you had invested just a hundred dollars back then, you would have about nine billion dollars today."

"Damn. wish I'd have been around to invest some money back then"

"Vida Costilla was Alexus' grandmama," Markio went on, crossing his right ankle over his left one and interlacing his fingers behind his head. "She heard about the Medallion Fund and invested seventy grand from her family business. She pulled out some years later, when her investment had increased to two hundred million dollars, and she used that to start MTN. Herb jumped on that same investment as soon as Papi told him about it. He was just a military man, didn't have a whole lot to invest, but he threw in nine thousand and forgot about it until my auntie came across the paperwork sometime in the late nineties. He had a few hundred million by the time they finally decided to pull the whole investment, but I think he's a billionaire now."

"He's a *billionaire!*" Morena's red-veined eyes got big again. She had just restarted the movie, but now she paused it again. "Are you telling me that man is a billionaire and he's risking it all just to come after you?"

Markio's mouth stretched open in a jaw spasming yawn. He could almost feel the digested Percocets working in his brain, numbing the neurons, ushering him toward an undoubtedly restful night of sleep. He nodded his head at Morena's question.

"He and my auntie, they practically own Hillside, Illinois. I think they own like two hundred houses and apartment buildings in that lil area alone. Auntie Bane and my mama moved into the Seylor House about a year ago. It's a big Spanish mansion way out there in Los Angeles, in the Los Feliz neighborhood. Auntie bought it from Aaron Paul, ol' boy from *Breaking Bad.* Aberdeen Avenue. They say Angelina Jolie lives right up the street."

Morena shook her head on Markio's shoulder, he hadn't realized she'd laid her cheek there until that very instant.

Their focus shifted to the movie, neither of them speaking. Ten minutes later Markio was struggling to keep his eyelids open. He was just about to tap out when Morena said, "Who's your top five?"

"What?" He had to blink his eyes awake.

"Your top five rappers of all time, dead or alive. Who are they?"

It took Markio five seconds to realize that, on his obnoxiously large TV screen, Chris Rock had just been asked the same question, and another five seconds to formulate an answer.

"Twista ... uh ... Crucial Conflict-"

"Wait, isn't that a rap group? How many people is that?"

"Four. Cold Hard, Wildstyle, Kilo, and Never. But they count as one." Markio rubbed a hand down his face. "Let me see, uhh, Twista, Crucial Conflict, Do or die, Da Brat, and King Von."

"You're just picking people from Chicago."

"I'm from Chicago," Markio reasoned.

Morena sucked her teeth. Her eyelashes tickled the skin on Markio's left shoulder as she rolled her eyes. He smirked at her attitude and found the breath to chuckle but was too tired to use it. The last thought that flashed through his mind was that Loochie had gotten a few limbs severed in his formal introduction to Herbert T. Harris. *I need to go and check on my nigga in the morning*, Markio thought.

Two seconds later he was fast asleep.

Chapter 20

Located on the north end of Millenium Park in downtown Chicago, the forty-two story office building constructed of dark glass and black steel that was now headquarters for iKiss Kosmetics had been owned and operated by a Chinese investment firm called Xing Lee Futures until Trump';s crippling tariffs forced them to invest elsewhere. With more than three hundred thousand square feet of office space, as well as a 4,400-square-foot members-only restaurant, state-of-the-art recreational facilities, childcare for those who needed it during their eight-hour shifts, and a ghost of other coveted amenities, iKiss HQ employed more than twelve hundred Chicagoans at salaries so competitive that Whiteny had yet to hear of anyone absconding to a better place of employment.

The morning after the most upscale hotel in her hometown was bombed to perdition; iKiss CEO Whitney Clarrett was seated behind the wide Egyptian mahogany desk in her top-floor office suite; simultaneously examining a mysterious tear in the cuticle of her left middle finger and trying to remember if she'd made any mistakes in meeting up with Nubby last night.

She'd picked the location herself, Evergreen Plaza on 95th and Western, way out on the far south Side. She'd had Flocka drive her there in his candy green McLaren coupe, and she'd handed the bag of cash through her window. Sure, Nubby had climbed out of his pickups and stood outside Whiteney's door in that weary empty parking lot, stood there with tears in his eyes and grief in his words as he recounted the Lighthouse Mall shooting and all the ways it went wrong, but Whitney had never gotten out of the car, and she'd worn a Pacers cap pulled down tight on her head with the bill hiding her face. She'd argued with Flocka all the way back to her condo, as he'd been pissed to learn that she was behind the brazen attack on his drug connect, but there was nothing she could do about that. The important thing was that she kept herself from even being mentioned in last night's deadly spate of shootings. She couldn't go on portraying herself as a victim if she got herself mixed up in a murder-for -hire investigation targeting the very person she was accusing of victimizing her.

Content with the state of her manicure, she went back to stalking her children's social media pages on her desktop computer. The twins, Eva and Ava, were flaunting their flawless figures on the foredeck of someone's yacht just off the coast of Malibu, California. Joselyn was already posting bedroom mirror selfies from the condo eight blocks north of iKiss HQ. Jimmy and his wife were absent from Instagram this morning, but their last post had showed them in the VIP Lounge at Queen of Diamonds Gentlemen's club, popping gold bottles of champagne and throwing up great snowstorms of cash for the dancers in their section.

Next up was Millionaire Markio's page. He was up to seven million followers now, many of whom were posting worried messages beneath his photos and videos, asad faces and broken hearts and praying hands, because the world-renowned novelist/screenwriter hadn't posted a single thing since the Slauson brothers were murdered last week.

"I wish it would've been you," Whitney muttered coldly.

There was a knock outside her thick walnut door. She looked up from her computer and said, "Come in," and in walked Trina Arnold, the beautiful transgender homegirl who'd been with her the night she was kidnapped by Markio's crew of depraved henchmen.

"Morning, boo," Trina said, bumping the door shut with her hip. Today the executive assistant wore a cream colored skirt that quit at the knee and a light green blouse that might have been silk. The belt she wore around her enviously narrow waist was a four inch wide length of black leather with a gold Chanel buckle. Her lustrous black wig was forty inches long and straight as silk with a perfect middle part. The open-toe pumps on her feet were green and fashioned from the skin of some unfortunate snake, and though they had six inch heels, she walked in them as if they were sneakers.

"You're late," Whitney said with half a grin.

"Bitch, don't start with me. You don't know what I had to go through just to get out the house for work." Smiling with glossy lips and a mouthful of perfect white teeth, Trina dropped her big fake butt into one of the two light blue leather chairs that faced the front of Whitney's desk at an angle. Her handsome round face, brown like Jiffy peanut butter, was one large smile. She had an iPad and an iPhone in one hand and a Starbucks cup in the other. "My Significant other seems to think I'm cheating every time I leave the fucking apartment. We just had a whole blowup. See?" She showed Whitney a webbed crack in the upper right corner of her phone screen. "He snatched my phone and threw it at the wall and everything. I'm surprised it still works."

Whitney rolled her eyes and shook her head. "You like that toxic shit." She left Instagram for the MTN News website and picked up her own cup of Starbucks coffee. It had gone cold, but there was enough sugar and caramel vanilla creamer in it to offset any bitterness in taste. "You see the news?"

"Girl, yes. My cousin Marketa was at that hotel last night. She had just flew in from Texas. I was just on the phone with her not even twenty minutes ago. She said the explosion shook that whole building."

"One of Joselyn's friends knows the girl they're saying was taken from the lobby of that hotel. She's from Texas, too. Houston, I believe. Her brother is Officer Gaing."

"Did you see the video of that old man leaving that hotel lobby?" Trina sucked her veneers. "He ain't kidnapped nobody. That he got in the car with him, *very* voluntarily. Hell, she opened his door for him."

And Trina was right. The news media had spun Vielle Gaing's involvement as a possible kidnapping, but Whitney knew better than that. She'd spoken with Harmonique Evans, who'd spoken with Herbert Harris. Vielle was still with him, and she could leave whenever she felt like it, but Whitney didn't think she would. According to Joselyn's old schoolmate, Bambi Middlebrooks, Vielle was a bonafide gold digger, and Whiteny knew from news reports that the old man had lots of gold to dig up. He was tight with his money like most old geezers, but he was probably willing to give up a little to the right kind of woman.

Judging from the photos of Vielle that had been floating around on social media since late last night, she was the right kind of woman for any heterosexual man with a healthy appetite for the opposite sex.

Vielle Gaing was a beauty, dead eye or no dead eye.

"Chop and Sherelle saved Loochie's life," Whitney said, staring at a photograph of the charred Bentley sedan that had been found burning on a back street in Hammond early this morning, just two blocks east of the Illinois state line where Calumet City began.

"I know," Trina said. "Marketa's brother was there. He helped hold Loochie down while they tied off his wrist and his leg to stanch the bleeding. Shit, that old man is some'n else, ain't he? I'd hate to be on his bad side. Markio fucked up pissing him off."

Markio

Whitney hated even hearing his name.

153

"I hope Herb blows his ass up next," she said, speaking her mind.

"Oh, he will. One thing you can say about that old man is he's very persistent. Sooner or later he's gonna find Markio, I'd bet my life savings on that, and when he does … Hm. I don't even wanna think about it."

But Whitney *did* want to think about it. Thinking about it made her nipples harden behind the earthy brown bustier-style top of her form-fitting Miu-Miu bodysuit. She could see the headline now: *Car Bomb Blows Millionaire Markio to a Million Pieces!*

The image made her giggle and grin.

After that she and Trina switched topics to the business of iKiss Kosmetics. Although Whitney's sister, Candace, had managed the company in her absence and was still overseeing most of the deals while also being solely in charge of the Department of Product Development and research, Whitney wasn't going to let herself just sit back and do nothing. Her mental health was in a dizzying tailspin most days, a whirl wind that could only be soothed with wine and pills and weed, but she was the CEO of one of the cosmetics industries leading black-owned businesses, and she'd be damned if she wasn't going to be kept in the loop.

There was a lot of information to absorb. As Trina began sifting through the emails, Whitney learned that iKiss Kosmetics was now available in over a thousand Walmart stores nationwide; that the company was facing nineteen lawsuits from customers alleging that iKiss products had harmed them in some way; that Candace had gotten a building permit approved to build an iKiss store in New York City, their third brick-and-mortar location on the East Coast.

While Whitney sat there behind her desk, listening to Trina and drinking her cold cup of coffee, she kept moving her computer mouse across the mouse pad, clicking in and out of different websites and applications in search of any new leads on Markio.

She found something new on World Star Hip Hop. the video, captioned *"Millionaire Markio Gifts Single Mom $25K,"* showed Twanika Marsh standing in her driveway with tears streaming down her face and seven or eight cheery-eyed children standing around her legs: the cash Nika had cradled against her stained shirt looked like a lot more than twenty-five thousand dollars. Whitney figured the rubber-banded bundles were made up mostly of twenties. Maybe there were even some tens thrown in to fatten the piles.

Whitney watched the first few seconds of teh video and moved on to the next WSHH post, which also had Markio's name in the caption.

"Vice Lords show Up In Droves To Support Millionaire Markio Following Reports That His Car Was Shot At Sunday Morning."

It was this second video that really made Whitney Clarrett grind her teeth together and scowl like a madwoman.

The video showed dozens of vehicles riding up and down West 16th Street in Chicago's North Lawndale neighborhood. Challengers, Chargers, Darangos, and Trackhawks; Bentleys, Benzes, and Beamers; Rolls-Royce, Ferraris, and Lamborghinis. The sidewalks were crowded with young black pedestrians, many of them with their hats cocked to the left of their heads, many of them raising their hands with the pinkie and ring fingers curled down and the other three raised to form the Vice Lord hand sign. Even the girls threw it up. Every other car played rap music with the volume cranked all the way up to the point of distortion. FBS pendants dangled from chains and dreads hung freely from heads. Whitney knew the area because she'd been there with Markio twenty or thirty times when they were dating. It was the west side neighborhood he was born and raised in, the neighborhood all the locals called Holy City.

"What are you over there watching?" Trina asked.

Whitney didn't answer. She was too busy thinking. The same teenage friend who'd told Joselyn about Vielle had also told her about Nubby's brutal murder. It was no real secret that Whitney and Nubby had messed around back in the day.

How long would it be before Markio made the connection?

Whitney's jawline hardened as her expression abruptly shifted from a petulant scowl to a look of grim determination. The heat was on, and there was no better time to turn it up than now. Two months ago she'd taken $1.2 million out of her bank account and stacked it neatly away in the wall safe she'd had installed in her home office. She'd given Nubby a hundred grand, and another $140, 000 had gone to less fortunate friends she'd grown up with in Michigan City, but there was still $960, 000 left inside that stainless steel cube, cash that could readily be used to end Markio once and for all; if she needed more than that, her bank was just a few blocks west of her condo.

Trina got up and came around to see for herself what Whitney was watching.

"Them Vice Lords love that nigga, don't they?"

Whitney didn't reply; she dropped a heavy breath out of her nose and said nothing.

"Y'all need to just forgive each other and let bygones say bye and be gone," Trina said, returning to her chair.

"Ain't no forgiving what he did to me," Whitney replied, the venom on her tongue poisoning her lips. "He had his friends rape me, Trina. They raped me, and then they tortured me."

"Had he been there, he wouldn't have let them touch you. I know that. *You* know that. Had you not started trippin' over the money he found in a storage locker that *he* paid for none of that shit would've happened. Y'all probably be married by now."

"Half of that money was mine."

"No the fuck it wasn't. You *wanted* half of that money to be yours, but you and I both know that it was never yours to begin with. That's what started this whole shit. Oh, and by the way, Nubby's big ugly ass sister is telling everybody that you're the reason her brother got killed. She told my cousin Kela that you called Nubby at work and paid him to quit his job and drive over to the Lighthouse Mall to try and kill Markio, which is when Nubby's son got killed, and she said Nubby had just handed her a bag of money he got from you when those boys pulled up and killed him."

Fresh tears sprouted from Whitney's tear ducts like water from a squeezed sponge. *Shit*, she thought, and pounded her fist on the desk.

"Yeah," Trina said. "Y'all need to forgive each other and figure all this shit out together before y'all both end up in prison. You got way more money than him now anyway. If you wanna be mad at him, kill him with success. Which you've already done."

Whitney sniffed twice and knuckled the tears from her eyes. "I'm going to jail," she cried. "I'm going to fucking jail."

"No you ain't. Girl, the shooters, one of the shooters took the bag when Precious dropped it. That's why she so mad. And besides, how they gon' say you knew Markio was at a mall in Michigan City when you were way out here in Chicago?"

That was a fair point. There was no way anyone could prove her knowledge of Markio's whereabouts yesterday morning. They'd have to know that the crooked Haitian cop was in cahoots with Herb, and that Herb had sent a photo of Markio and the crooked cop to Harmonique's phone, and that Harmonique had then forwarded the pic to Whitney's phone. That was a lot of speculation.

All these thoughts were racing through Whitney's head when her secretary, Pam Sturgis, appeared in her open doorway. Pam knocked as if the door was closed. Behind her stood Terrance "TJ" Jones, a former offensive lineman for the Chicago Bears that Trina had hired on as Whiteny's personal bodyguards. He was carrying a cardboard box in front of his clean black suit, and when Whitney, dabbing her eyes dry with a Kleenex, looked up and nodded for them to enter, TJ walked in and placed the box on her desk.

"It's for you," Pam said. "The woman who delivered it to the front desk asked that it be delivered to you immediately, said it was important, so I sent TJ down to get it."

Rising from her swivel chair, Whitney furrowed her brow. The box was taped shut. Someone had written FOR WHITNEY CLARRETT on the top of the box in red permanent marker. She took a letter opener from her desk drawer and cut through the tape. When she opened the flaps her lips fell apart.

There was cash in the box. Bundles upon bundles of hundred dollar bills, all bound together with rubber bands, red ones and blue ones and brown ones too. A yellow Post-It note was stuck to Benjamin Franklin's forehead on one of the cash piles.

$2.5 million, the note read.

Trina started laughing.

Chapter 21

"… Where Herbert Harris was spotted four hours ago crossing over into Mexico from a port of entry right here in Hidalgo, Texas. What you are seeing on the right side of your screen is a video of Harris that a bystander was able to capture as she and Harris crossed the bridge on foot. Harris was last seen entering a black Ford SUV with an unknown black female driver. He is believed to be traveling under the alias Jesse James Harris, which is the name of his deceased brother. Anyone with information regarding Harris' whereabouts is encouraged to contact the Federal Bureau of Investigation at …"

Markio pressed the power button on his TV remote and watched the screen of his 212-inch television go black. He had the urge to grab his iPhone and wasted a few minutes scrolling through social media, but his son, MJ was sitting next to him watching cartoons on it. Morena's four-year-old, Manolo, was engrossed in the same animated show on his mama's phone, kicked back at the other end of the sofa with his bare feet crossed at the ankles, and from where Markio sat on the big white couch he could look back and see Morena standing out on the balcony, smoking a blunt of OG Kush and watching a dark family of storm clouds roll in from the eastern horizon.

With a noisy grunt and an exaggerated groan that made the boys giggle, Markio used the soft leather arm of the sofa to haul himself to his feet, and from there he walked out to join his favorite nurse on her smoke break.

"I knew you were a weedhead the first day we met," he said, and he chuckled merrily when Morena regarded him with a hard side-eye. "What? I'm lyin'? You were higher than a muhfucka, first few times we met."

Morena rolled her drooped eyes and took another long take on her weed-stuffed cigarillo. "This is some really good Kush." She held the blunt out in front of her and squandered a moment admiring it. Then she swung her arm in Markio's direction. "Here. Hit it."

He accepted the blunt and puffed on it. He'd fallen off the sobriety wagon five nights ago, when he took those two Percocets and drank some of Slime's Lean, and since then he'd smoked somewhere between thirty and forty blunts with Morena and the gang.

Black Reggie was out of jail. The prosecutor had declined to file charges against him for defending himself against the men he'd shot. The guy he'd wounded was now being charged with murder for the death of the other Ft. Wayne gunman, as well as another charge of attempted murder for a woman Reggie had accidentally shot in the shootout. It was the way the law in Indiana worked.

Whitney had showed up on 16th Street shortly after Morena delivered the cardboard box full of cash to iKiss Headquarters. There wasn't much conversation, but Whitney had smiled, and Markio had smiled, and the two of them were seen hugging and speaking in several photos and videos that had instantly gone viral.

The next day, shortly after returning to Michigan City, Markio and Morena were pulled over in his snow white Bugatti Veyron by three MCPD patrol cars. They had sat there on the side of Michigan Boulevard - Morena covertly sliding her registered Glock pistol from under Markio's right thigh and stashing it in her gator-skin Gucci bag, Markio sweating like an ancient Egyptian slave and trying not to appear too nervous - until a dark blue Chevy Tahoe with police lights painted inside the headlights arrived on scene, and out of that Tahoe stepped a tall, slim, terra-cotton brown MCPD detective named Hardis Gaing Jr. the detective handcuffed Markio and shoved him into the backseat of the Tahoe. Morena was ordered out of the Bugatti, and seconds later a tow truck had taken it away.

Thirty minutes after that Markio was sitting in an interrogation room at the Michigan City Police Department, a dimly lit box of a room with a dingy brown carpet, vapid blue walls, and two fluorescent tubes on the ceiling for light. One of the tubes glowed weakly, and its parallel twin worked in sporadic flickers.

Markio sat in a padded steel folding chair the same color as the walls behind a small square table made of imitation weed. He had been patted down for weapons, but they hadn't taken his phone, so he used it to phone his lawyer.

"I'll be there in ... forty minutes," she'd said. "Sit tight and don't say a word. Let me see if I can reach the mayor's office."

The door swung inward and Detective Gaing entered the room just as those last two words were spoken. A cold sneer of a grin flashed across the cop's brownish-orange face and then it was gone, faster than Markio could blink.

Gaing appeared to be in his late twenties or early thirties, much too young to be a detective in any major city, but apparently just right for a city of thirty thousand denizens. His hair was black and shiny and brushed into waves that span all around his head. His eyes were hazel orbs of hatred, and he had a peculiar slanting scar on the left side of his neck. His shirt was silver, his tie was blue with thin gray diagonal stripes, and his pants were navy blue.

"The mayor's office, huh?" Gaing sat down across the table from Markio. The middle finger on his left hand had a small round bump on the left side of the middle knuckle. He began tapping that callus on the edge of the table. "The mayor's office ain't gonna help you outta the shit storm you're in, I can tell you that now."

Markio stuck out his lower lip and breathed, exercising his right to remain silent.

"We know it was you who killed Nubby and his boys in front of Precious Tucker's place, just like we know it was you who killed Nubby's son earlier that day. That's a death sentence, you know that? One Park Row. Remember that address? Indiana State Prison. I'm sure those guards you assaulted will be more than happy to welcome you back."

Markio smiled, tilted his head to the side, and shook it ever so slightly.

"You go on smiling, motherfucker. We'll see if your Hollywood friends can get you off death row. See if Kim Kardashian'll petition the governor on behalf of a no good Chicago gangster. I don't think she will." Gaing sat forward, brought his elbows to rest on the table, and glowered at his captive. "I'll tell you this much," he said in an ice cold whisper. "If that uncle of your harms so much as a hair on my sister's head, I'll be paying you a visit. You hear me?"

"That nigga ain't my uncle."

"He's married to your aunt."

"I wouldn't give a fuck if he was married to my mama. It don't make him no kin to me. I don't like that nigga just like you don't like him, and if I knew where he had your sister, I would go and get her and bring her to you. Not for you but for your pops. Whole time I knew that man he was solid."

Gaing stared at Markio for a full minute, saying nothing at all. He stroked his incipient goatee as if it were a full-grown beard. Markio though the looked like a real street nigga who had woke up that morning and decided to be a cop.

"Why'd you kill Nubby?" Gaing asked, after the chin-stroking bout of silence. "Precious told us it was you, ya know."

"Am I under arrest?"

"Way she tells it, Whitney Clarrett paid Nubby to quit his job and go after you, and when Little Nubby shot at your car, you shot back and killed him. That was your motive for killing Nubby and those three Chicago boys later that night, am I right? You had to get to him before he got to you."

"Am I under arrest?" Markio asked again

"Not yet. But you will be. You can bet your bottom dollar on that."

"I can't even find my bottom dollar. Too many dollars piled on top of it," Markio replied as the detective got up to leave the room.

Celebrity attorneys Niddia Staples and Britney Bostic, of the prestigious Bostic and Staples law firm, had escorted Markio out of the police station an hour and ten minutes later, and Markio had paid a local moving company to pack up all of his belongings from teh Beachwalk Lane property and transport it all back to his Lincoln Park home in Chicago.

Yesterday evening, Markio, Morena, and their two sons had boarded a Gulfstream 650 jet and flown down to Miami Beach, Florida, where, on an affluent stretch of Collins Avenue, the Costilla Resort Hotel head recently opened for business. They were in the Matamoros Suite, which spanned the entire 62nd floor, just below the penthouse. Markio had paid the full amount for a one year lease of the luxury condominium, which at $160, 000-a-month was a significant amount of money - almost two million dollars.

He held in the weed smoke for as long as he could and then blew out in one hard stream. The time on his rose gold and diamond Rolex watch was 3:27 pm, early afternoon, but the bevy of approaching storm clouds had blotted out the sun, turning day into night. Those clouds were like great black muscles with lightning for veins, or at least that was how Markio saw them. The feathery white cirrus clouds that had streaked the blue dome of the sky half an hour earlier were long gone.

"And you say you got this place for a year?" Morena asked, restarting a conversation they'd had two days ago. Markio nodded, and she said, "This is, hands down, the most beautiful apartment I've ever seen in my life. It's like a smaller version of your place in Chicago. How much did it cost you?"

"Not much." Markio took another drag on the blunt and passed it back to her. "It got a deal."

He hadn't gotten a deal on the place. He was being modest. Maybe he could have gotten a deal if he'd spoken with Alexus before the purchase, but Queen A hadn't spoken with him since Whiteny accused them of having her kidnapped and tortured. Alexus was on the road with her husband, multiplatinum gangsta rap artist Blake "Bulletface" King, whose 71-city Mob Boss Tour had already grossed north of $800 million globally. Markio and the rapper had become pretty good friends over the past couple of years, and he supposed that, over a few blunts and a cup of lean, he could have negotiated a better deal on the lease, but since money wasn't an issue, he hadn't tried it.

"I wish I knew how to write a movie, or a book somebody could turn into one," Morena said. She yanked down the ham of her tight black leather Chanel minidress, which fit her like latex. A single raindrop, pushed sideways by a westerly wind, alit on the tip of her nose as she tilted her head back and sucked more smoke from her weed stick. "I could write about all the crazy men I had to deal with working at that prison. There were some real creeps. I mean *creepy* creeps."

"I know. I been there before."

"You've done time at New Castle, the prison?"

Markio nodded. "Not that long, though. I was at the Annex, it's kinda like a step-down program for niggas they label too violent for general population. They sent me there from the SHU after I beat this white boy's brains out with a lock. Nigga fucked up a ninety-thousand-dollar play."

"Oh, no. That's not New Castle I mean it is, but it isn't. The Annex is a totally separate prison from general population. Population is where they house the sex offenders. Freakiest men you'll ever meet in your life." she shivered at the thought. "*God*, I hated working there."

Markio chuckled at the sight of her disgusted grimace. More rain fell, dotting their skin in a steadily increasing drizzle. Markio wore a white T-shirt with a gold Fendi design running down the front, from his left shoulder to his right hip, in a wide diagonal stripe. A stripe of the same width and color made up the hem of his white cotton shorts, the pockets of which were bulging with cash. His Fendi sneakers were also white-and-gold.

Before the rain became too intense, they went back inside, shut the glass sliding door, and returned to the sofa. Morena wedged her extinguished blunt in an ashtray on the coffee table and used the remote to turn on *Shrek*. You couldn't lose with *Shrek*. The kids handed over their parents' iPhones as soon as the grumpy green ogre appeared on the screen.

There were five others in the condo with them: Slime, Brittany, two housemaids, and a personal chef named Selena Bilby who was just as stunning and curvaceous as her cousin Morena. Selena's Colombian mother and Morena's Colombian father were siblings, and although Morena had inherited a decent level of South American culinary skill, Selena had mastered the craft.

Slime and Brittany had started up some kind of sexual friendship that involved way too many lubricants and sex toys for Markio's taste. During an early morning shopping spree they'd gone on seven or eight hours ago, while Markio and Slime were perusing the merchandise at a high-end designer clothing store on Lincoln Road, Brittany had asked Morena to walk with her to an adult toy store half a block away. They had returned with seven bags of items that included eight different kinds of lubricants; two vibrating cock rings; a throat-numbing spray to bypass their gag reflexes and assist them in deep throating; an assortment of vibrators, including a few that could be inserted vaginally and controlled using a phone app; several dildos of varying girths and lengths; and a few other items that Markio didn't get to see. Selena had been in the kitchen preparing brunch for them, when they got back to the condo, but Slime and Brittany had only given her a very brief greeting before rushing off to the guest bedroom they'd chosen when they made it in last night. It was ten o'clock when they retired to that bedroom. Markio hadn't seen or heard from them since.

"Aren't you glad I talked you into giving Whiteny that money?" Morena asked as he sat there beside Markio, studying the side of his face while he replied to a text message from his older cousin Tweety.

"Hell yeah," he said. "Whatever it takes to get her to stop mentioning my name to the feds. Had they raided my spot in Lincoln Park a few days earlier, I would've got popped off with all kinda shit. Fully automatic choppas, Glocks with switches and drums, pints of the higher ups at the FBI on her payroll. She had Enrique warn me just in time to get all that shit outta there."

"Isn't Enrique her old bodyguard?"

"Yeah, that's him." *And now he's in charge of her drug cartel*, Markio thought to himself, but of course he couldn't say that to Morena or anyone else. He didn't even feel comfortable mentioning Enrique Aleman. He wished he hadn't. "But yeah, Whitney, Whitney's good people. I didn't expect her to pull up and give me a hug, but it was definitely a good look."

"Aren't you worried that the police might figure out what happened at that mall?"

Markio shook his head. "It was self-defense."

"Yeah, but you left the scene of a crime and failed to report it."

"I don't report crimes."

"You're really crazy, you know that?"

Markio cut a suggestive grin at Morena. She sucked a tooth, fingered a tress of hair from in front of her forehead, and rolled her eyes. She then looked at MJ with surprise when the three-year-old ripped the TV remote from her grasp to turn up the volume.

Thirty seconds later Markio and Morena left the boys with their movie and departed the living room for the master suite they'd broken in the previous evening. To get there they had to traverse a long, broad hallway made entirely of rich white marble. In fact, most of the condo was constructed of white marble and glass. Open doors and doorless entryways on either side of the hall left into three other bedrooms, a vast white kitchen with a huge white marble center island, an enormous dining room (where Selena, clad in a tight pink T-shirt and tight blue pants that only appeared to be made of denim, was busy arranging plates and spoons and forks for the dinner she was cooking), a cigar room, a game room, a room filled with exercise equipment, a four chair hair salon/barber shop, a room with a front-loading washer and dryer stacked one on top of the other, and two big bathrooms that were in addition to the five adjoining bathrooms in each of the bedrooms. The two housemaids – a lanky, coffee-black woman in her mid to later forties and a homely, heavyset Cuban woman who was perhaps ten years younger – were cleaning in one of the big white bathrooms, while Chief Sosa sat a few feet away, watching them wipe down the walls and sink. He looked back when he scented Markio and Morena walking past the open doorway behind him, and then he got up and came hopping after them.

Macabre screams of a dying young white woman issued forth from Brittany and Slime's closed door. Morena paused there a moment to listen, and when she laughed the horror stopped and Brittany yelled out, "Hey! You nosey motherfuckers!"

Markio cracked up laughing, and they continued on toward the end of the hallway, striding past gold-framed 12X12 photos of rap artists that Markio himself had chosen when he first paid the one-year lease. There was Kodak Black, Chief Keef, Twista, Lil Durk, Yo Gotti, Jeezy, and EST Gee on one broad hallway wall, and Gucci Mane,

GloRilla, NBA Youngboy, Bump J, G-Herbo, Polo G, and Bulletface on the opposing wall.

It felt like they'd walked a mile when they finally entered the monochromatic suite that more closely resembled a luxury hotel room than a black man's actual living quarters: Everything was white, from the gold veined marble walls and ceiling to the frilled leather drapes hanging down in front of the nine-foot-high windows. The sheets, blanket, and pillows could have been molded from fresh white snow. There was no visible bedframe outside of the four squat white legs that held the gigantic Alaskan-King bed off the floor. Plush white rugs flanked the bed on three sides. Snakelike LED lights extended downward from the ceiling, baking the room in bright white light. Even the frame of the two-hundred-inch widescreen television was milk colored.

All that heavenly white made Morena's three red bags of sex shop goodies stand out like sore thumbs in the middle of the bed.

"I still can't believe this is my life," Morena said, raising her iPhone to capture a quick video of the room for her Instagram Stories.

"I still can't believe you think we're about to use whatever you got in them bags," Markio countered.

"Boy." An eye roll accompanied the word. She flapped her wrist dismissively and continued filming. "Everything in there is for me, and trust me, you're gonna love seeing me put it all to good use."

"I'm just sayin'. I ain't Uncle Elroy. You ain't 'bout to have me werin' no leather mask, beatin' me with no whips. On the gang."

Markio laughed as he fell back onto the bed, and Morena laughed with him as she climbed on top of him. A sudden crash of thunder made her flinch, and that got them laughing harder.

"Scary ass," Markio said, thinking that maybe, just maybe, he'd finally found The One.

Epilogue

The End Of The Road

Three months later ...

Markio ended up donating a million dollars to a GoFundMe that had been set up for the victims of the hotel bombing, and another hundred grand to the GoFundMe that Sherrelle, Loochie's longtime girlfriend, had set up for the cost of his medical care.

Markio chose the twenty-first day of September, 2025, a sun-drenched Sunday in Miami Beach, to kneel down in the sand and offer Morena a sparkling platinum twelve carat diamond engagement ring. He'd hired a professional photographer to capture the indelible moment, and immediately afterwards they'd boarded a private jet to Chicago, where their family and friends were gathered for a surprise engagement party at his Lincoln Park mansion.

Now, exactly one month and one day later, as Markio stood out on the sky-high balcony of his Miami Beach condo, taking big puffs from a hefty blunt of exotic bud and considering the plotline to a screenplay he'd been working on for the past few weeks, he stared vacantly off to the side of the building, at another tall structure full of condominiums.

"Baby, did you call your mom back?" Morena asked from the living room behind him.

"Yeah, I called her. She didn't want nothin'. Her and Auntie Bone just bored in that big house they got, need somebody to talk to, that's all." His voice sounded heavily congested from all the smoke he was holding in his lungs. His eyes strayed from the neighboring building, and he looked straight ahead at all the glittering white yachts and cruise ships that dotted the rippling cobalt waters beyond the marina.

A minute or two of blessed silence passed. Then Morena, who was still the same droopy-eyed marijuana, connoisseur she'd been when they met back in July, appeared next to him and promptly plucked the blunt from between his fingers.

While she smoked he stood there appreciating the hot sun on his face and arms. Today he wore a yellow-and-white Amiri T-shirt over matching shorts and Nike Air Max '95 shoes. His only jewelry was the watch. Morena was dressed down in a simple red crop-top and a pair of blue-and-white biker shorts that fit her so tightly it seemed she was smuggling two hale hams in the back of them.

Markio reached over and squeezed one of those hams.

"You think Herb's ever coming back?" Morena asked, after a time."

"I don't know Shit, he might. Ain't no tellin' with his old ass. That nigga like a black cat - he got nine lives, and he bad luck all around the board."

Morena snickered. "You should stop writing fiction and start writing true stories about *your* life. I bet that shit would sell out so fast."

"Brittany still in New Orleans with Slime?"

"No, they left yesterday. He got them backstage with NBA Youngboy. She said the New Orleans police superintendent just banned YB from performing in Louisiana because he kept going out there on Bourbon Street after the concerts."

"You done got my cousin to fall in love with a snow bunny."

"They're good for each other. Maybe she'll keep him out of trouble, keep him from going back to prison."

Markio couldn't argue with that, so he didn't.

They finished smoking and retired to the living room, where there were no children to manage this particular morning. MJ was back home in Chicago with his uncle Bam, and Manolo was in Maryland with his grandmother from his mother's black side of the family. Morena had a long list of siblings and cousins with children her son's age, and many of them other lived with or spent most of their free time with Granny Manfield in Laurel Maryland. Markio was only three months into his relationship with Morena, and he'd been to Granny Manfields place five times already.

Ensconced in the luxurious comfort of an obnoxiously overpriced white leather sofa, Markio and Morena snacked on candies from her purse and let *The Real Housewives of Atlanta* watch them as they talked about their plans for opening a restaurant in West Baltimore's Lexington Terrace neighborhood. Morena had already gotten the go-ahead from Baltimore Mayor Brandon Scott, and Markio had purchased the building just last week. Months of construction lay ahead, but they were on the right path.

"You're the greatest," Morena said, and kissed him square on the lips. "Thank you so, so much. You don't know how much this means to me."

Markio smiled a beaming smile and breathed a sigh of supreme contentment. He kissed her back, rubbed between the thighs of her biker shorts until her mouth fell open in a tremulous inhalation, and then sat back as she dug his dick out of his shorts and stuffed as much of it in her pretty mouth as she could fit.

That Wednesday in October was a remarkably good day.

Little did either of them know, the good times would be cut short rather abruptly, and Markio wouldn't live to see their wedding day.

The End.

Lock Down Publications and Ca$h Presents
Assisted Publishing Packages

Due to an increase in the price of services we have increased our prices. The prices below reflect the price increase as of 11/1/24.

BASIC PACKAGE **$699** Editing Cover Design Formatting	**UPGRADED PACKAGE** **$1000** Typing Editing Cover Design Formatting Upload eBooks to Amazon Upload Paperback to Amazon
ADVANCE PACKAGE **$1,400** Typing Editing (line editing/content) Cover Design Formatting Copyright Registration Proofreading Upload eBooks to Amazon Upload Paperback to Amazon	**LDP SUPREME PACKAGE** **$1,700** Typing Editing (line editing/content) Cover Design Formatting Copyright Registration Proofreading Set up Amazon Account Upload eBooks to Amazon Upload Paperback to Amazon Advertise on LDP's Amazon and Facebook Page

***

Other services available upon request.
Additional charges may apply

Lock Down Publications
P.O. Box 944
Stockbridge, GA 30281-9998
Phone: 470 303-9761
Email: lockdownpublications@gmail.com

Submission Guideline

Submit the first three chapters of your completed manuscript to ldpsubmissions@gmail.com. In the subject line add **Your Book's Title**. The manuscript must be in a Word Doc file and sent as an attachment. Document should be in Times New Roman, double spaced, and in size 12 font. Also, provide your synopsis and full contact information. If sending multiple submissions, they must each be in a separate email.

Have a story but no way to send it electronically? You can still submit to LDP/Ca$h Presents. Send in the first three chapters, written or typed, of your completed manuscript to:

LDP: Submissions Dept
P.O. Box 944
Stockbridge, GA 30281-9998

DO NOT send original manuscript. Must be a duplicate. Provide your synopsis and a cover letter containing your full contact information.

Thanks for considering LDP and Ca$h Presents.

NEW RELEASES

BLOODLINE OF A SAVAGE 1-3
THESE VICIOUS STREETS 1-3
RELENTLESS GOON 1-3
BY PRINCE A. TAUHID

THE BUTTERFLY MAFIA 1-3
BY FUMIYA PAYNE

A THUG'S STREET PRINCESS 1&2
BY MEESHA

CITY OF SMOKE 3
BY MOLOTTI

GET IT IN SLUGS 1 &2
BY B. STALL

STANDING ON HER BUSINESS 1&2
BY DG SANTANA

STEPPERS 1,2&3
THE REAL BADDIES OF CHI-RAQ
BY KING RIO

THE LANE 1&2
BY KEN-KEN SPENCE

THUG OF SPADES 1&2
LOVE IN THE TRENCHES 2
CORNER BOYS
BY COREY ROBINSON

TIL DEATH 3
BY ARYANNA

SUPER GREMLIN 5 | KING RIO

THE BIRTH OF A GANGSTER 4
BY DELMONT PLAYER

PRODUCT OF THE STREETS 1-3
BY DEMOND "MONEY" ANDERSON

NO TIME FOR ERROR
BY KEESE

MONEY HUNGRY DEMONS 1-2
BY TRANAY ADAMS

HUB CITY MENACE 1-3
BY J. WHITE

A THUGGISH PASSION 1&2
LAND OF DA HOOLIGANZ 1-4
KILLAZ ON STANDBY 1&2
BY IRA B.

FO'EVA ROLLIN 1&2
BY ASSA RAYMOND BAKER

THE LEVEL UP 1&3
BY LUXURY KING

Coming Soon from Lock Down Publications/Ca$h Presents

IF YOU CROSS ME ONCE 6
ANGEL V
By Anthony Fields

A THUGS STREET PRINCESS 3
By Meesha

CORNER BOYS 2
By Corey Robinson

THA TAKEOVER
By Keith Chandler

BETRAYAL OF A G 2
By Ray Vinci

SAVAGE FAMILY EMPIRE 1&2
SOULLESS GOON 1,2&3
THE DIRTY SIDE OF MONEY 1,2&3
By Prince

FOR MY ENEMY'S SAKE
AMBITIONS OF A SLIDER
FRESH OFF DA PORCH
By IRA B.

BY THE TRUCKLOAD 1-4
TIPPIN' THE SCALES 1-3
BAD BITCHES WIT GUNZ 3
PROBLEM SOLVED 2
By Christopher "Diesel" Hornezes

Available Now

RESTRAINING ORDER 1 & 2
By **CA$H & Coffee**

LOVE KNOWS NO BOUNDARIES 1-3
By **Coffee**

RAISED AS A GOON I, II, III & IV
BRED BY THE SLUMS I, II, III
BLAST FOR ME I & II
ROTTEN TO THE CORE I II III
A BRONX TALE I, II, III
DUFFLE BAG CARTEL I II III IV V VI
HEARTLESS GOON I II III IV V
A SAVAGE DOPEBOY I II
DRUG LORDS I II III
CUTTHROAT MAFIA I II
KING OF THE TRENCHES
By **Ghost**

LAY IT DOWN I & II
LAST OF A DYING BREED I II
BLOOD STAINS OF A SHOTTA I & II III
By **Jamaica**

LOYAL TO THE GAME I II III
LIFE OF SIN I, II III
By **TJ & Jelissa**

IF LOVING HIM IS WRONG…I & II
LOVE ME EVEN WHEN IT HURTS I II III
By **Jelissa**

PUSH IT TO THE LIMIT
By **Bre' Hayes**

SUPER GREMLIN 5 | KING RIO

BLOODY COMMAS I & II
SKI MASK CARTEL I, II & III
KING OF NEW YORK I II, III IV V
RISE TO POWER I II III
COKE KINGS I II III IV V
BORN HEARTLESS I II III IV
KING OF THE TRAP I II
By **T.J. Edwards**

WHEN THE STREETS CLAP BACK I & II III
THE HEART OF A SAVAGE I II III IV
MONEY MAFIA I II
LOYAL TO THE SOIL I II III
By **Jibril Williams**

A DISTINGUISHED THUG STOLE MY HEART I II & III
LOVE SHOULDN'T HURT I II III IV
RENEGADE BOYS 1-4
PAID IN KARMA 1-3
SAVAGE STORMS 1-3
AN UNFORESEEN LOVE 1-3
BABY, I'M WINTERTIME COLD 1-3
A THUG'S STREET PRINCESS 1&2
By **Meesha**

A GANGSTER'S CODE 1-3
A GANGSTER'S SYN 1-3
THE SAVAGE LIFE 1-3
CHAINED TO THE STREETS 1-3
BLOOD ON THE MONEY 1-3
A GANGSTA'S PAIN 1-3
BEAUTIFUL LIES AND UGLY TRUTHS
CHURCH IN THESE STREETS
By **J-Blunt**

CUM FOR ME 1-8
An LDP Erotica Collaboration

SUPER GREMLIN 5 | KING RIO

BLOOD OF A BOSS 1-5
SHADOWS OF THE GAME
TRAP BASTARD
By **Askari**

THE STREETS BLEED MURDER 1-3
THE HEART OF A GANGSTA 1-3
By **Jerry Jackson**

WHEN A GOOD GIRL GOES BAD
By **Adrienne**

THE COST OF LOYALTY 1-3
By **Kweli**

BRIDE OF A HUSTLA 1-3
THE FETTI GIRLS 1-3
CORRUPTED BY A GANGSTA 1-4
BLINDED BY HIS LOVE
THE PRICE YOU PAY FOR LOVE 1-3
DOPE GIRL MAGIC 1-3
By **Destiny Skai**

A KINGPIN'S AMBITION
A KINGPIN'S AMBITION II
I MURDER FOR THE DOUGH
By **Ambitious**

TRUE SAVAGE 1-7
DOPE BOY MAGIC 1-3
MIDNIGHT CARTEL 1-3
CITY OF KINGZ 1&2
NIGHTMARE ON SILENT AVE
THE PLUG OF LIL MEXICO 1&2
CLASSIC CITY
By **Chris Green**

SUPER GREMLIN 5 | KING RIO

A GANGSTER'S REVENGE 1-4
THE BOSS MAN'S DAUGHTERS 1-5
A SAVAGE LOVE 1&2
BAE BELONGS TO ME 1&2
A HUSTLER'S DECEIT 1-3
WHAT BAD BITCHES DO 1-3
SOUL OF A MONSTER 1-3
KILL ZONE
A DOPE BOY'S QUEEN 1-3
TIL DEATH 1-3
IMMA DIE BOUT MINE 1-6
DYING FOR LIKES
By **Aryanna**

A DOPEBOY'S PRAYER
By **Eddie "Wolf" Lee**

THE KING CARTEL 1-3
By **Frank Gresham**

THESE NIGGAS AIN'T LOYAL 1-3
By **Nikki Tee**

GANGSTA SHYT 1-3
By **CATO**

THE ULTIMATE BETRAYAL
By **Phoenix**

BOSS'N UP 1-3
By **Royal Nicole**

I LOVE YOU TO DEATH
By **Destiny J**

I RIDE FOR MY HITTA
I STILL RIDE FOR MY HITTA
By **Misty Holt**

180

SUPER GREMLIN 5 | KING RIO

LOVE & CHASIN' PAPER
By **Qay Crockett**

TO DIE IN VAIN
SINS OF A HUSTLA
By **ASAD**

BROOKLYN HUSTLAZ
By **Boogsy Morina**

BROOKLYN ON LOCK 1 & 2
By **Sonovia**

GANGSTA CITY
By **Teddy Duke**

A DRUG KING AND HIS DIAMOND 1-3
A DOPEMAN'S RICHES
HER MAN, MINE'S TOO 1&2
CASH MONEY HO'S
THE WIFEY I USED TO BE 1&2
PRETTY GIRLS DO NASTY THINGS
By **Nicole Goosby**

LIPSTICK KILLAH 1-3
CRIME OF PASSION 1-3
FRIEND OR FOE 1-3
By **Mimi**

TRAPHOUSE KING 1-3
KINGPIN KILLAZ 1-3
STREET KINGS 1&2
PAID IN BLOOD 1&2
CARTEL KILLAZ 1-3
DOPE GODS 1&2
By **Hood Rich**

THE STREETS ARE CALLING
By **Duquie Wilson**

STEADY MOBBN' 1-3
THE STREETS STAINED MY SOUL 1-3
By **Marcellus Allen**

WHO SHOT YA 1-3
SON OF A DOPE FIEND 1-4
HEAVEN GOT A GHETTO 1&2
SKI MASK MONEY 1&2
By **Renta**

GORILLAZ IN THE BAY 1-4
TEARS OF A GANGSTA 1/&2
3X KRAZY 1&2
STRAIGHT BEAST MODE 1&2
By **DE'KARI**

TRIGGADALE 1-3
MURDA WAS THE CASE 1-3
By **Elijah R. Freeman**

SLAUGHTER GANG 1-3
RUTHLESS HEART 1-3
By **Willie Slaughter**

GOD BLESS THE TRAPPERS 1-3
THESE SCANDALOUS STREETS 1-3
FEAR MY GANGSTA 1-5
THESE STREETS DON'T LOVE NOBODY 1-2
BURY ME A G 1-5
A GANGSTA'S EMPIRE 1-4
THE DOPEMAN'S BODYGAURD 1&2
THE REALEST KILLAZ 1-3
THE LAST OF THE OGS 1-3
By **Tranay Adams**

MARRIED TO A BOSS 1-3
By **Destiny Skai & Chris Green**

KINGZ OF THE GAME 1-7
CRIME BOSS 1-4
By **Playa Ray**

FUK SHYT
By **Blakk Diamond**

DON'T F#CK WITH MY HEART 1&2
By **Linnea**

ADDICTED TO THE DRAMA 1-3
IN THE ARM OF HIS BOSS
By **Jamila**

LOYALTY AIN'T PROMISED 1&2
By **Keith Williams**

YAYO 1-4
A SHOOTER'S AMBITION 1&2
BRED IN THE GAME
By **S. Allen**

TRAP GOD 1-3
RICH $AVAGE 1-3
MONEY IN THE GRAVE 1-3
CARTEL MONEY 1&2
By **Martell Troublesome Bolden**

FOREVER GANGSTA 1&2
GLOCKS ON SATIN SHEETS 1&2
By **Adrian Dulan**

TOE TAGZ 1-4
LEVELS TO THIS SHYT 1&2
IT'S JUST ME AND YOU
By **Ah'Million**

SUPER GREMLIN 5 | KING RIO

KINGPIN DREAMS 1-3
RAN OFF ON DA PLUG
By **Paper Boi Rari**

THE STREETS MADE ME 1-3
By **Larry D. Wright**

CONFESSIONS OF A GANGSTA 1-4
CONFESSIONS OF A JACKBOY 1-3
CONFESSIONS OF A HITMAN
CONFESSIONS OF A DOPE BOY
By **Nicholas Lock**

I'M NOTHING WITHOUT HIS LOVE
SINS OF A THUG
TO THE THUG I LOVED BEFORE
A GANGSTA SAVED XMAS
IN A HUSTLER I TRUST
By **Monet Dragun**

QUIET MONEY 1-3
THUG LIFE 1-3
EXTENDED CLIP 1&2
A GANGSTA'S PARADISE
By **Trai'Quan**

CAUGHT UP IN THE LIFE 1-3
THE STREETS NEVER LET GO 1-3
By **Robert Baptiste**

NEW TO THE GAME 1-3
MONEY, MURDER & MEMORIES 1-3
By **Malik D. Rice**

CREAM 2-3
THE STREETS WILL TALK
By **Yolanda Moore**

SUPER GREMLIN 5 | KING RIO

THE STREETS WILL NEVER CLOSE 1-3
By **K'ajji**

LIFE OF A SAVAGE 1-4
A GANGSTA'S QUR'AN 1-4
MURDA SEASON 1-3
GANGLAND CARTEL 1-3
CHI'RAQ GANGSTAS 1-4
KILLERS ON ELM STREET 1-3
JACK BOYZ N DA BRONX 1-3
A DOPEBOY'S DREAM 1-3
JACK BOYS VS DOPE BOYS 1-3
COKE GIRLZ
COKE BOYS
SOSA GANG 1&2
BRONX SAVAGES
BODYMORE KINGPINS
BLOOD OF A GOON
By **Romell Tukes**

CONCRETE KILLA 1-3
VICIOUS LOYALTY 1-3
BLOODY MONEY BAGS
By **Kingpen**

THE ULTIMATE SACRIFICE 1-6
KHADIFI
IF YOU CROSS ME ONCE 1-3
ANGEL 1-4
IN THE BLINK OF AN EYE
By **Anthony Fields**

THE LIFE OF A HOOD STAR
By **Ca$h & Rashia Wilson**

NIGHTMARES OF A HUSTLA 1-3
BLOOD AND GAMES 1&2
By **King Dream**

GHOST MOB
By **Stilloan Robinson**

HARD AND RUTHLESS 1&2
MOB TOWN 251
THE BILLIONAIRE BENTLEYS 1-3
REAL G'S MOVE IN SILENCE
By **Von Diesel**

MOB TIES 1-7
SOUL OF A HUSTLER, HEART OF A KILLER 1-3
GORILLAZ IN THE TRENCHES
OOPS CRY TOO 1&2
THE DAUGHTER OF A CARTEL BOSS
By **SayNoMore**

BODYMORE MURDERLAND 1-3
THE BIRTH OF A GANGSTER 1-4
By **Delmont Player**

FOR THE LOVE OF A BOSS 1&2
By **C. D. Blue**

KILLA KOUNTY 1-5
TENDER
By **Khufu**

MOBBED UP 1-4
THE BRICK MAN 1-5
THE COCAINE PRINCESS 1-10
STEPPERS 1-3
SUPER GREMLIN 1-4
A GANGSTA'S SON
By **King Rio**

MONEY GAME 1&2
By **Smoove Dolla**

SUPER GREMLIN 5 | KING RIO

A GANGSTA'S KARMA 1-5
By **FLAME**

KING OF THE TRENCHES 1-3
By **GHOST & TRANAY ADAMS**

BAD BITCHES WIT GUNZ 1&2
PROBLEM SOLVED
By "Christopher Diesel" Hornezes

QUEEN OF THE ZOO 1&2
By **Black Migo**

GRIMEY WAYS 1-3
BETRAYAL OF A G
By **Ray Vinci**

XMAS WITH AN ATL SHOOTER
By **Ca$h & Destiny Skai**

KING KILLA 1&2
By **Vincent "Vitto" Holloway**

BETRAYAL OF A THUG 1&2
By **Fre$h**

COUNTDOWN OF A KILLA 1&2
SEX, MURDER AND GOD 1&2
GUNS DOWN, BOTTOMS UP 1&2
By Lo-Life

THE MURDER QUEENS 1-7
By **Michael Gallon**

FOR THE LOVE OF BLOOD 1-4
By **Jamel Mitchell**

SUPER GREMLIN 5 | KING RIO

HOOD CONSIGLIERE 1&2
NO TIME FOR ERROR
By **Keese**

PROTÉGÉ OF A LEGEND 1,2&3
LOVE IN THE TRENCHES 1&2
By **Corey Robinson**

THE PLUG'S RUTHLESS DAUGHTER 1&2
By **Tony Daniels**

BORN IN THE GRAVE 1-3
CRIME PAYS
By **Self Made Tay**

MOAN IN MY MOUTH
By **XTASY**

TORN BETWEEN A GANGSTER AND A GENTLEMAN
By **J-BLUNT & Miss Kim**

LOYALTY IS EVERYTHING 1-3
CITY OF SMOKE 1-3
By **Molotti**

HERE TODAY GONE TOMORROW 1&2
By **Fly Rock**

WOMEN LIE MEN LIE 1-4
FIFTY SHADES OF SNOW 1-3
STACK BEFORE YOU SPLURGE
GIRLS FALL LIKE DOMINOES
NAÏVE TO THE STREETS
By **ROY MILLIGAN**

PILLOW PRINCESS
By **S. Hawkins**

SUPER GREMLIN 5 | KING RIO

THE BUTTERFLY MAFIA 1-3
SALUTE MY SAVAGERY 1&2
By **Fumiya Payne**

THE LANE 1&2
By Ken-Ken Spence

THE PUSSY TRAP 1-5
By **Nene Capri**

DIRTY DNA
By **Blaque**

SANCTIFIED AND HORNY
by **XTASY**

BOOKS BY LDP'S CEO, CA$H

TRUST IN NO MAN
TRUST IN NO MAN 2
TRUST IN NO MAN 3
BONDED BY BLOOD
SHORTY GOT A THUG
THUGS CRY
THUGS CRY 2
THUGS CRY 3
TRUST NO BITCH
TRUST NO BITCH 2
TRUST NO BITCH 3
TIL MY CASKET DROPS
RESTRAINING ORDER
RESTRAINING ORDER 2
IN LOVE WITH A CONVICT
LIFE OF A HOOD STAR
XMAS WITH AN ATL SHOOTER

www.ingramcontent.com/pod-product-compliance
Lightning Source LLC
Chambersburg PA
CBHW071209260626
47162CB00004B/1238